Malicious Intentions

WORKS BY SYK KELLY

CRUEL GODS SERIES:
BRINGER OF DEATH

CRUEL KINGDOMS SERIES:
SINISTER DESIRE
FATEFUL CHANCE
MALICIOUS INTENTIONS

CRUEL KINGDOMS

Malicious Intentions

SYK KELLY

DEDICATION

For all the wicked ones who don't hold their tongue and do what they want with their middle finger high. There's a Devil out there who doesn't think you're too much.

CONTENT WARNING

This is a dark romance novella containing the following trigger warnings: spanking, sub/dom dynamic, forced piercings, bondage, cock warming, attempted sexual assault, physical assault, parental abuse, murder, poisoning, manipulation, torture, forced abortion (not detailed).

Chapter One

I always knew I would die young.

A prophet once attempted to read my palm before clocking the subtle violet within my honey-toned eyes.

Wicked, she labeled me. *Witch. Evil. The Devil's Child.*

I didn't disagree with the last one. My father is the Devil reincarnate. When I told him what the woman called me, he forced her to bow at my feet before kissing each one with distressed apologies.

The poor woman had no idea of the gift she gave me that day. I was so raptured by her sureness that I was meant for nefarious things that at the ripe age of seven, I was reborn. No longer Amelvira Lunasol Aramos, the girl whose father used her to dazzle his friends with my moonlit-blonde hair, unique eyes, and perfect smile, but Mel, the girl who marveled at seeing those who harmed or insulted me put in their place. It wasn't the power my father thrives for that ignited something in me, it was a righted wrong, the balance of it—the karma.

On our way out, the woman grabbed my arm and whispered a string of incoherent, cursive ramblings into my ear before promising that being daddy's little girl was only going to cause me great misery. "Listen well, Satan's Spawn, for every evildoing you put forth, every curse you spill, may your grave be riddled with spikes for double requite."

MALICIOUS INTENTIONS

This moment of my rebirth is what I remember as I die. My body burns with a fire I can't see, needling pain laces through my skin and into my bones, searing the bloody streams flowing through my veins. My head thunders with a thousand lightning bolts, and when I open my eyes, my heart lurches out of my chest as I'm met with the face of the Devil.

Not my father, the actual Devil is staring at me while I'm slowly burning hotter in whatever rings of Hell my body belongs to. His eyes are voided blacks like a depthless cauldron. His disheveled white hair leaves a lock draped above his brow as if pointing exactly where I'm supposed to remain lured, but it's the black ink along his neck that tears my attention away, the strange symbols that run down the side of it to where his red tunic is unbuttoned and a white birthmark begins.

Only a devil could cause me such fervor.

"I..." My voice cracks from disuse. "I know you."

From a dream, or rather a nightmare. There's a familiar gleam in his soulless eyes that's telling me it's the latter, though I'd be lying if I said I don't hope it's a titillating version of the former.

"Yes, you do, wicked one." His lips lift only enough to speak before settling back into the hateful glare.

It's the last two words he says that have me looking deeper into my surroundings. There are no cavernous fire pits or stalagmite that spear through my body after all. I'm lying on a small bed, my arms covered in white gauze. The room is simple, wooden walls with a small table layered with more white gauze, bloody rags, a bin, water, mortar, pestles, salve tins and vials.

I know a witch's lair when I see one. Maybe that's it. The Devil found me and is making me his personal little witch. I'm not humble. I wouldn't be surprised if my talents with a mortar and pestle are superior enough to catch the attention of the divine.

The man leans further back, kicking out his feet and crossing his ankles as he takes his time rolling his sleeves to his elbows, revealing fresh, deep, and bruised scars along his arms.

The sight has a memory flash before me. It's him, lying in a round chaise with the same relaxed posture he has now, only he wasn't looking at me then. It's too fast of a glimpse to recall anything else except the same flush rushing beneath my flesh that's heating my cheeks now.

Spotting water on the nightstand, I do my best to sit up while my back screams for me to remain still. Not one to listen, I bite through the pain, my jaw clenched as I settle against the headboard. A soft groan escapes at the brush of warm sensitivity tickling down the side of my spine. Whatever happened to my arms, the worst is on my back.

The man watches me struggle without a single ounce of expression on his face or an inkling of wanting to help.

"Where am I?" I ask, grabbing the water and finishing it before he says a word. At this moment, I'm truly angry that magic doesn't exist because the first thing I would do is turn this rubbish into wine.

"Deep in the forest where no one will find you." His lips kick up. "Or hear you."

My stomach rattles. That gleam in his eyes returns, and now I know he's fucking with me. Except...

"You want me to what?" I'm shouting, sure he can't mean what he just said.

Dragon's head tilts, the scales on his mask glimmer from the golden sunset. "We can't let this wedding happen, Devil Doll. Killing him is the only way. Can you do it, or are you too deep?"

I shake my head furiously. "No. Of course, I can do it. Hayse is a monster."

"What do you remember?" The Devil's voice pulls me from the distant memory until I'm locked back into those black voids.

Hayse—not the Devil at all, but the man I was supposed to kill, scowls at me in a way that makes my blood boil and my body quiver. I don't *quiver* for anyone. Not out of fear, lust, hate… Whatever happened, my body remembers a mix of emotions my mind can't.

"Silent for once?" He leans forward, his elbows resting on his knees. "Fine. Let me tell you how this is going to work. You're not leaving until I say so. You're not shackled here, but don't tempt me. You won't run away or answer the door for anyone. Understood?"

The second I start to cross my arms, he stands from his chair and steps forward, grabbing my wrists and pulling them to my sides as if I'd insulted him. All the blood rushes to my head, making the room blur as he leans over me. "I asked if you understood."

"Why?" My voice cracks. Something must have gone wrong while killing him. Maybe he found out and decided to get to me first, kept me alive only so I could be aware of whatever torment he has laid out for me.

"Because," he lets go with a dismissive toss and steps back, raking his fingers through his hair, "we're *both* wanted for murder, wicked one."

We? My head spins. If I didn't kill *him*, then who in the hell did I kill?

Chapter Two

This has to be a joke.

"You're telling me this old *woodcutter's* cottage only has skimpy, lacy lingerie?"

After Hayse made valid arguments that he could have murdered me in my sleep if he genuinely wanted me dead, I slowly got my bearings. *Very* slowly. Whatever happened to me was brutal. My entire body is riddled with scars that look like someone tortured me with tiny needles and razors. If I didn't have the savage training my father put me and my siblings through, I'm positive I would have fainted from the purgatory that now resides in my body. A rib is definitely broken, my leg is sprained, my wrists ache, and my head is fucked, considering the missing memories.

The sinister side of me would make a joke about being as unstable as my sister, Eva, but those are intrusive thoughts I would never voice. She's the saint to my sin, no matter how many voices she hears or people she hallucinates.

"He must have had his go around the harlots." Hayse gives a lazy shrug as he reaches for a black silk slip. It's not until we're both standing that I take in how tall he is. He may not be a devil, but he is a monster. I'm on the smaller side and he's at least a foot taller than I am. Even standing a few feet away, I can see that the top of my head *might* come to his shoulders without my usual heels.

He notices me taking him in and smirks. Unlike all the other arrogant bastards, his comes with a depravity that has the memories thumping against my temple, begging to be released. "It's the silk in my hand or the tweed on my back." His fingers tease a button on his tunic and then the next, the white birthmark growing longer and wider.

He's watching me with curious interest, like a cat pawing at a hanging toy. Whatever game he's playing, I can play, too. Life is but a game, and I've won every challenge thrown my way.

Untucking the sheets wrapped around me, I hold the edges out to my sides for a second before letting them drop at my feet, motioning my impatient hand for him to hurry this along.

Seeing as how I woke up stark naked, he's already seen me nude, but I wouldn't know it from his reaction. The asshole has the gall to throw the slip back in the wardrobe as he lowers his gaze, assessing every battered inch of me without any shame. "Wicked as always."

I make a point to keep my eyes on his as he pulls his shirt over his head and takes the five steps toward me to place it into my waiting palm. "Now, why don't you do something useful and cook us breakfast? I like pancakes and coffee."

As he stalks out the door, I get the slightest glimpse of more tattoos that cover most of his back: one long black wing and more symbols and sigils I can't make sense of.

Shimmying into his shirt, I'm taken aback by the scent of bergamot and blackberries. Ignoring the calming scent, I scoff and shout to him, "I can cut a carrot or heat up oats. Take your pick."

Walking from the bedroom to the tiny kitchen takes most of my energy with every limp I inch toward it, but it's all worth it once I find the decanter on the counter. "I know vintage is your preference." He sounds proud of himself.

"It's morning." Isn't it? That's what he said, and every shutter is closed with a chill that tells me it's likely the crack ass of dawn.

"The time of day has never stopped you before." There's oddly no judgment in his tone, and when I begrudgingly offer him a glass, he waves me off. "I don't drink."

I eye him with more suspicion. People who don't drink either have a past or are annoyingly religious. His tattoos say the former and pique my interest a little more.

As I take my first sip, I watch him closer. He doesn't plop onto the couch like most do, but lowers himself, telling me he's a patient man. My father forced me to notice these things. A tick of a jaw, a raise of a brow, the parting of lips; they're all easy tells as to how one is feeling, but watching someone move in routine tasks like sitting, eating, or even walking reveals so much more.

I don't bother with a glass when determination and agony fuel me to finish the whole thing. I swipe the decanter and sit opposite him, crossing my legs in the chair and taking in my new prison. There's not much to it; the red-bricked chimney is boarded up, there's a coffee table with too many coffee rings, the small tan couch Hayse sits on, and the overly soft chair I'm comfortable enough in. The walls are bare, one with an actual tree growing out of it, and there isn't another door that leads anywhere except the washroom visible in the corner and the one with too many locks that must lead to outside.

How quaint. I take a long sip from my personal decanter. "We both better pray there's more of this here." I take three more long pulls, savoring the dry tannins on my tongue.

Hayse leans forward, pulling something out of his pocket. He's so fast it's hypnotizing to watch him sprinkle the brown petals of tobacco and dreamroot into the paper and roll it with gentle precision before flicking a match off his knee. Lifting the flame, he lights the spliff that hangs from his lips behind a cupped hand. A puff of smoke fills the air as his free hand rests between his legs.

It takes physical effort not to take in the rest of him. His tattoos and muscles peeking through where his new, black top doesn't cover don't tell me much except that he works hard to sculpt himself perfectly and that he takes pain well, might even enjoy it. Vain—this man is the epitome of vain.

The scent of his vice intermixes with mine and takes me to a hazy, lax state of mind.

"So, tell me," I start. "Who did we kill?"

His lazy gaze flickers to mine.

"You tell me. You're the one who—"

Pounding on the front door startles us both. Hayse is on his feet, his hand wrapped around my mouth before I can think to say a single word, let alone scream. His breath is hot against my ears, so close I can taste the sweet and bitter herb. "Don't make a fucking noise, or we're both dead."

I reach up and pinch his nipple, feeling the metal pierced through it behind the fabric. That doesn't stop me from twisting it for good measure so he backs off. "I'm not an idiot," I mouth back.

To anyone else, trusting their enemy might seem ridiculous, but I know myself too well. If this man says we killed someone, I don't doubt it. He has no tells of a liar, just an intense loathing, which is reasonable considering I was instructed to kill him.

We might hate each other, but neither of us wants to die.

The pounding starts again, less enthusiastically.

Without a care about my injuries, he shoves me aside to settle snuggly beside me, returning his hand tightly against my mouth. If my skin and bones weren't blazing with sharp stings and aches with every movement made to secure his position, I would attempt to fight him off, but I'm too damaged to put up any struggle, let alone a good one.

"What's the last thing you remember?" There's a need behind his question as he releases my mouth enough to reply.

I won't tell him about my task to take him out, so I tell him about my sister Eva, how she was attacked after her impromptu wedding and arrived at my brother's. She was still healing when I left for the Deimos Kingdom.

After a long silence, he stands and heads for the kitchen, grabbing a knife and tucking it behind his back, then another in his boot. "I need to follow them to see who that was." Disappointment radiates off his stony expression. "Rules?"

"Don't leave or answer the door," I answer so fast I'm taken aback. What the hell was that? I'm not a dog. I don't sit, bark, or play dead.

"Do you roll over, too?" He snickers to himself as he unlatches both locks. "Since you can't cook, why don't you use that spinning wheel thing in the corner? Make me something nice."

My cheeks burn as hot as my core. Seriously, what is in this wine? No woman or man alive has ever affected me so heatedly. I've never wanted to burn someone alive, revel in their body flaying over a spit, while equally wanting to hate fuck them until my bones are screaming.

"Why don't you sit on that pointy spindle, and I'll show you—" The door shuts, cutting me off.

Gaping asshole.

If he thinks I'm going to sit here and twiddle my thumbs, cook, or use that damn wheel, he doesn't know the first thing about me.

I don't bother to look around while he's gone. This clearly isn't his home, and he's not the type of man to leave me to my own devices if he has something secret hidden away. I don't even bother to look for pants once I open the door and confirm that we are, in fact, deep in the woods.

The sun isn't out, yet the heat is thick with summer, the trees are full, and the grass is lush, all of which means I haven't lost too much time, maybe a few weeks of memories. Everything was bare when my sister was attacked, and I met with Dragon and the Trove.

I'm no tracker, but there's a clear path veering off to the right that I follow. The worn grass, more soil than the green blades, soothes my sore feet. Every hobble reminds me of the old burns on the bottom of them from when my father forced Eva and me to dance in burning heels as a poetic lesson to never follow our brother's footsteps and marry for love. We're to marry to strengthen the kingdom, forge alliances, anything to bring the Aramos name to high regard and hold the highest power.

All of that now resides on my shoulders since my brother, Cain, married a harlot he fell in love with, and Eva married the Damned Prince, who she was apparently sent to kill. I guess my little saint isn't completely holy, though she didn't go through with the murder.

I shake all thoughts of the future away, as always, and focus on my task at hand.

The rush coursing through me at doing exactly what Hayse told me not to is the pain reliever I need. With every step, I'm less aware that I was tortured or fell off a cliff. The pain quickly turns into adrenaline, and instead of hobbling, I'm softly sprinting down the worn path, my ears on alert for any strange noise, my eyes peeled for any sudden movement.

Within seconds, I'm so sweaty that my black ring, big enough to sit on three of my fingers, starts to slip off. I fist my hands to keep it secure. It's the only material thing I'll ever treasure, besides the medicine inside of it.

As a clearing in the distance comes into view, I slow, hearing a loud splash erupt in the distance. I whip my head to the right, where it came from, spotting the river glistening through the trees.

What in the hell is this man up to?

I spot his pants, shirt, and boots, wet, muddy, and hanging over a thick branch.

My stomach kicks with the familiar feral flutters that usually lead me to trouble. But there's no scene to cause here. No one to witness my most natural self, except Hayse.

This is child's play.

Taking every piece of clothing into my arms, I walk closer to the river, finding him waist deep, running his hands through his hair to clean off the mud caked within the white. Even with the brown tint, he's devastating to look at. His stiff jaw is set with irritation, his cheekbones are sharp, and his body is chiseled to perfection.

None of that keeps me from holding in my laugh at the realization he fell into mud. His head whips to me at the sound, angling with a wry shake. "No treat for you."

"Oh, *this* was treat enough. What happened? Fall into mud, or did that mysterious knocker attack you?" I hold his clothes high, so he knows I have all the power here.

His half-cocked grin humbles me quickly—there's a first time for everything. "If you wanted to see me naked, all you had to do was beg. Preferably on your hands and knees."

He would find a way to take all the fun out of this. The lower part of his V is dangerously close to the surface as he moves toward me. The scars that pepper every inch of his warm ivory skin are so similar to mine, yet he doesn't show any hint of pain.

Again, I know myself too well to stick around for the temptations that are clouding my mind. The old me must have had a reason not to kill him, because right now, I can't see a reason I would do anything other than ravish him.

Turning on my heels, I run for my life. My heart thumps faster with every step, hearing his footsteps padding behind me.

He's fast. I wouldn't have thought him able to get out of the water so quickly.

MALICIOUS INTENTIONS

Keeping my focus on the trail ahead is irritatingly difficult with the image of him running behind me completely naked, obscuring my concentration. My imagination paints a vivid scene that literally makes my stomach tickle.

I'm ready to give in, craning my neck back to see how accurate I am, when arms wrap around my shoulders. My back slams against a tree so hard my head bounces off the trunk with a *crack*.

My vision is black before the blur fades, and I'm face to face with someone who isn't Hayse.

"How did you find me?"

Dragon's mask tilts to the side, keeping me pinned tight against the tree. "Playing house?"

"No," I snap. "Something happened." I motion my hands up and down my body, showcasing the scars, as best as I can with his grip on my shoulders. "The last thing I remember is meeting you—"

"Find his ring first. If you still want to kill him, do it. I won't stop you, but only after you find his ring."

"Ring?" I ask. I would have noticed him wearing a ring. I'm drawn to out-of-place things, and a ring on a man is one of them.

"The amethyst ring. Find it!" Dragon's voice rises. "Do whatever it takes to get it. Do you understand?"

What is with men asking me if I understand? I'm not a dog, and I'm certainly not an imbecile. Do they think I'm ill in the head? Certainly I've made my reputation otherwise.

"What's so important about this ring?" I know better than to ask questions, but I can't help it when questions are all I have. A ring is sentimental. What could Dragon or the Trove possibly want with it?

"Find a way to get your memories back, and you'll know." His head whips back at the sound of approaching footsteps. "You have a week to decide if you can trust him or kill him. But if you don't find that ring, you're out of the Trove for good."

Chapter Three

It's been one day, but it feels like months. I've searched this damn cottage twice over, and there's no amethyst ring. Hayse doesn't wear any jewelry except the ones through his nipples. Since I stole his clothes at the river, he's taken a liking to wearing nothing but briefs that leave absolutely nothing to my overworking imagination. I'm almost positive he has jewelry there too, and I swear, if it's the amethyst, I'm up for the challenge of retrieving it.

I may need to search for signs that he infused a desires draught in the wine because I can't seem to get a grip. Watching him draw into a notebook while lounging on the couch with a spliff hanging from his mouth, so unbothered and uncaring, is hot as hell.

I find many men attractive, women too, but there is something about him that's unnervingly beautiful—the white hair he shoves to the side, the black ink covering most of his body, the cut muscles that could destroy me in seconds, the brutal scars, his callousness… I was born with a weakness for things that could ruin me—body, mind, spirit, and especially my reputation.

Since neither of us can cook, dinner is the vintage red in my lap and the herbs burning his lungs. It turns out a heaping side of glaring is both of our favorite desserts, and we're indulging a little too much tonight.

He may be alluring, but a pretty face can't detour me from what I've wanted and worked years to be a part of: The Trove. It's the one place I yearn to belong to, though everything about me says otherwise. They rid the world of weeds in their perfect garden, silently killing the corruption in every kingdom, while all I've ever done is cause mayhem. I thrive in it. I guess that's why Duke, the leader, approached me to be their distractor. Their weapons contact, Dragon, had other plans for me, while my brother Cain, known as Death, rejected me fiercely. He was backed by Dove, their spy, who loathes me. Something about my eyes turns her away, like everyone else in this world.

Pussies.

My natural specialty is something my father exploited long ago, something that comes so naturally it's boring, but something tells me seducing Hayse will be anything but.

Shaking back my hair, I give a sultry pout. "If we have to stay here, at least entertain me. Don't you do anything interesting? Sing? Dance?" I bite my lip to keep from cursing myself for introducing such horrendous hobbies. If he says yes, all his attractiveness will dissipate with that one word. "Since you have no interest in telling me who we killed, the least you can do is make this prison a little less boring." I stand on my feet, swaying slightly from the vintage merlot. "You didn't even bother to cook me dinner."

"I put it in that stupid container to breathe." He juts his chin toward the empty decanter that's gone through two bottles today already.

His expression twists when he sees me leaning my palms on the counter behind me. I frown with another pout, letting his scarlet shirt rise higher along my thigh as my chest juts out a little more, tapping my sharp nails against the wood. "I didn't take you for someone so boring."

He tosses the notebook aside and rises to his feet. "Sit on the table." He doesn't take a single step, his eyes narrowing on me, waiting.

Anyone else would have dropped to their knees at the authority behind his order, but the brat in me won't let me move.

"Did I stutter?" His tone holds an edge of dominance that grips my spine, but there's something else too, something mean—*threatening*. "If I did, I'm sure you still would have understood the gist of what I said."

"I understood completely." It takes everything to tame my tongue into a careless cadence because I'm positive he'd only find a way to make another dog joke about me biting back at him. "It's your tone I don't care for. There was no *please* or—" The second I cross my arms, he moves, reaching me in three steps to pull them away from my chest, spinning me around so they're clasped behind my back. My feet are forced forward as he leads us to the tiny dining table for two nestled in the kitchen corner. He releases my wrists only to spin me back to face him.

"*Sit.*" His voice is softer this time, like sin rolled in satin with a hidden dagger nestles inside.

"I'm not a do—"

I shriek when he clasps the back of my thighs and lifts me onto the table with too much ease, stepping between my parted legs so I can feel him against the most intimate part of me. "Hayse!"

"I'll ask twice only once." His brow rises in question, begging me to test his patience so he can show me what happens if I don't heed the silent warning.

I nod without full comprehension of what he asks or what I'm agreeing to. All plans and sanity are wiped from my mind the second his stony features shift, revealing a smile that holds malicious intentions I desperately want to be on the receiving end of.

His fingers graze under my jaw. "Isn't it funny how your body remembers what your mind doesn't?"

I jerk my leg in a failed attempt to knee him in the balls; there isn't a way to in this position. The threat only has him tightening his hold on my thighs to keep them still. "See, we've been here before. You're going to fight me, so I'll punish you." He smacks where part of my ass hangs off the ledge. My knees jerk to tighten, but with him between me, I squeeze his waist instead. "But then that good girl inside of you takes over because *deep* down, you like it, being told what to do, being used, the punishment, the pain…"

My mouth barely has a chance to part before he's pinching my lips between his fingers. He doesn't say anything as his free hand slides down my shin. The sensitivity of every cut should hurt, should make me work harder to kick him off, but I'm putty in his palms as he guides each of my legs to opposite corners of the table. My top shifts, hiking over my waist, exposing me to him as he takes a seat and pulls my hips forward.

Holy Hell.

Don't get me wrong, I've had both men and women in every position imaginable, but I'm the aggressor. I'm the top. I'm the one controlling every movement, every word, everything. I have to be.

But this…

He lights another spliff, smoke rising between my parted legs. "What's wrong, wicked one? Devil splice your tongue?" He doesn't move, doesn't *do* anything. He's just watching me with those alluring eyes I refuse to look into.

"What's wrong with *you*?" I cock my head, taking the burning paper from his lips and placing it between mine. Inhaling, I let the thick herb roll around my mouth before letting it rush down my throat. I bring my hand to the back of his head and his white hair is silk between my fingers. "Does God have you repenting for sins you haven't committed yet?"

"Sins?" He snags the cigarette from my lips before wrapping his arms under my legs to grip into the thickness of my thighs. "Is it a sin to have Sunday dinner at the table?"

He digs his thumbs into my skin, widening my legs, his dark gaze lowering to my center brazenly. His lower lip rolls between his teeth before his eyes flicker back to mine.

I bite into my own lip to keep myself from ruining this.

My breath catches on the thick smoke as he bridges the gap between us, bringing his head where I've had a constant ache since waking in that bed. All I see is his white hair before he lifts back up with the spliff back between his lips, his head cocking to the side with a self-assured grin I want to slap off his face.

I'm ready for anything he sends my way. I'll degrade him. Maybe I'll praise him. Whatever it is, I'm hyperaware that he's about to say something that needs the sharp tongue I've been honing for years.

His words don't come.

His tongue doesn't either.

Smack!

My head snaps back, my throat letting out a sharp groan as his hand slaps what's exposed of my ass. "Your attempt at seduction isn't what put you on this table, wicked one. It's the fact that you had an ulterior motive written all over your face the second you leaned against that counter." I don't get a breath in before his fingers penetrate me, his knuckles settling deep with a thick pressure that has my entire body lax with submission.

"*Oh, fuck!*"

"Such sinful language." His hot breath teases against me before I feel his wet tongue against my thigh, his teeth grazing my injured skin with a piercing raptor that sends shivers through my flesh as his fingers move in and out of me at a slow, controlled, heavenly pace I never want to end. "What is it you thought would happen? That I would come over here, fuck you, and spill whatever secrets you're looking for because your holes are so heavenly?" His mocking chuckle enrages me because, yes, that's exactly right. Everyone spills their secrets in the throes of pleasure.

"Pl—" I swallow the plea in the back of my throat. I'm not here for him to get me off. "Tell me—"

"No," he snaps. "Hold this." He stops me before I can work my usual charm, raising his arm to place the spliff back between my lips. His tongue darts out, pressing against the top of my entrance, above where his fingers are working, dragging up millimeter by agonizing millimeter until finding the spot that has my mind forget everything that led us here. "I can taste the wickedness in you. All the lies and deceit."

The tickle against my backside has me sucking in the air through my teeth. "What—" My moan replaces the words as his fingers curl and his tongue swirls in the same rhythmic pattern. Most men switch everything up, trying new speeds and directions, but he knows... *fuck*, he knows...

"Hayse..." My hand falls back through his hair. "I don't think I can—"

Pounding at the door pulls me away from the man between my legs, who keeps lapping me up as if he didn't hear anything. If he doesn't care, then neither do I. "Hayse..."

"It's me!" A familiar voice pierces my heart.

Hayse drops my clit from between his teeth. "He'll stop in a second."

Pounding patters along the wooden door again, harder. "It's *me*."

Hayse's soulless eyes flicker to mine. He knows who that is too and he still doesn't stop. If anything, that voice has tightened his hold on me and his tongue has slowed to draw this out.

I'm on the edge, teetering, as the pounding continues. "Let me in, asshole!"

The growl deep in Hayse's chest pushes me over. I reach for my breasts, needing that stimulation, when I'm met with something foreign. Sharp metal is pierced through each one of my nipples.

I don't have time to think through this as a wave of quivering pleasure spreads through me, starting where his fingers pump without hesitation, the teasing against my backside…

Taking the spiked ends of each piercing, I pinch and pull, biting my lip harder to keep my whining moans deep in my throat.

I'm still riding the oncoming waves when Hayse disappears. His fingers leave me empty, his tongue leaves me cold, his entire presence abandons me as I'm riding nothing but the air on the table.

The locks unlatch too quickly for me to gather myself. My body is shaking, my breath is wavering as I lift myself to a sitting position—as if it's natural to be sitting on a table, flushed, in nothing but a man's top with a spliff between my fingers. He knows I don't smoke.

A figure steps through the door, his eyes wild, his tunic torn and covered in soot, and his dark hair is more disheveled than Hayse's. When his eyes land on me, they soften. "Mi Vera."

At Percival's words, memory after memory strikes me fast and hard.

What the hell have I done?

Chapter Four

One Month Ago

"Hey there, danger." The distorted voice behind the dragon mask puts a smile on my face.

"More like *doom* because she's fucking cursed." My brother, Cain, shoves his finger into Dragon's chest, not bothering to keep his voice low with this meeting deep in the vast forest outside of his home. "I don't know what you're looking for, but she isn't how to get it. All she does is cause problems."

His words should hurt, but a day hasn't gone by where my brother hasn't looked at me as if I pissed in his oats or fucked his wife. I do threaten to do things like the former and almost succeeded at the latter, so I suppose there is slight cause.

Something shifts in Dragon, like watching a literal dragon with scales that shimmer and wings that begin to spread with his broadened posture. "Says the man who leaves death in his wake." He catches my brother's wrists. "Why don't you go back to your pretty wife and mind your damn business?" He tosses Cain's hand to the side and gives his mask a flick on the nose.

Duke wraps his arms around Cain before he has a chance to reach for his dagger and murder their weapons supplier for being so daring. I'm tempted to say defensive, but no one has ever defended me.

Still, anyone who willingly throws themselves in the way of a man who calls himself Death has my admiration. I've heard rumblings about Dragon. He creates weapons that he tests personally. Every sword or dagger the Trove buys has been christened with blood by its creator.

I've met him twice in passing. Once, when he cornered me last year at my brother's ball to request a dream draught I created, and again when I delivered the mass amount at Princess Aspen Whitehart's ball weeks ago. Why he needed so much wasn't my concern, and he paid me generously not to ask questions.

"The Trove is my business," Cain shouts, shoving Duke off him and straightening his clothes.

All of this is so trivial. I look over my freshly painted nails and admire the shimmering aubergine sharp points while the territorial pissing match runs its course. It's these moments that I'm thankful I don't have a cock. Their poor little brains must be exhausted trying to figure out whose is bigger at every meet up.

"Then consider this no longer Trove business." Dragon's mask tilts towards me. "Do you want to help me or not?"

Before I can mutter a single thought, Duke steps between us. His usual calm demeanor vanishes behind his horrid, beastly mask as his overbearing size makes the trees around us feel smaller. He's a big man, tall and built like a warrior, but Dragon is equally intimidating in an entirely different way. His ability to remain silent and appear indifferent is a weapon in itself.

"Mel is *my* business." Duke's voice is level, but there's an underlying warning that warms my cold, little heart. "Which makes her the Trove's. You're not to harm her or let harm fall on her. Do you understand?" He doesn't let him answer before turning toward me. "For all transparency, I owed Dragon a no-questions-asked favor for saving my life. He chose *you* to help him."

"A temptress with thick skin is what I need," Dragon says matter-of-factly. Dicks are put away and it's all business now. "The man I need looked into requires a certain... *challenge* to hold his interest."

The emphasis on challenge sends rabid rabbits jumping through my stomach. I've never been so thrilled by a single word.

Duke steps aside, giving him a slight nod of approval. Dragon pushes off the tree to pull something from behind his back. I suck in the crisp morning air when I see the small, heart-shaped mask with tiny black horns emerging from the top. I catch it between my hands, admiring it closer. "This is mine?"

"Consider this your initiation." I can hear the smile behind Duke's mask and the groan behind Cain's. I've caused a few distractions for them in the past, but nothing so official. Nothing that earned me a mask. "Wear that when you meet and if you need an out—"

"I won't," I cut him off and lift the mask over my face. The smooth, polished finish hides it well, but there's an unmistakable dusty wood aroma that's never smelled so good, and the lace that covers the lower part of my face is a special touch that speaks to me.

Feminine, feral, and fatal.

Duke's heavy hand falls on my shoulder. "I'll find a way to check on you."

I'm ready to tell him not to bother, that there's nothing I can't handle, but as Duke and Cain start back toward the house, leaving me alone with Dragon to discuss what he needs, I hold my tongue. For the first time in my life, I *care* about succeeding at something, and the last thing I need is for my temper or loose tongue to mess this up.

"Damn." I might not be able to see Dragon's face, but I can feel him assessing me. From my long, silver-blonde hair to the tied bodice over my off-the-shoulder chemise that's tucked into my fitted leather pants, the black ring on my right hand, all the way to my laced-up boots with the pointed heels. When I'm not *impressing* royals, I prefer to slip out of the silk dresses, though I'll never stop adding a pretty flair to whatever I wear. My looks are my number one weapon after all.

"With that Hell's crown on your head, you look like the Devil's favorite doll."

"Cute," I drawl, tucking my arms over my chest while taking in his hooded, black cloak. It's the only thing I can see besides the dragon mask. "What's that make you? Her pet?"

His shoulders shake as if he's laughing, but no sound graces the air. "Keep this attitude. You'll need it when you gather every secret Hayse Soren has." That name prickles my ears, but I'm not sure why. I must have heard it before, but I can't place it. "His name has been of interest to overseas royals as of late. I want you to figure out why."

"That's it? Learn secrets?" Disappointment sours my mood. "Let me guess. Do what it takes. Use my body if I must." I roll my eyes hard enough that my head tips back. Typical. "This isn't a challenge. I'll have him singing me his mother's, brother's, and grandparent's secrets within a few hours."

"Oh, little doll, I promise you're wrong about that. Hayse isn't like most men, which is why I also want to ensure you stay close to him. Depending on the information you gather, he could be useful to us." As in the Trove. He leans against the tree with a shake of his head. "This outfit is doing it for me, but you'll want to pack the lace you keep for special occasions to impress Hayse. He plays in the Forbidden Den."

The air is sucked from my lungs as a tingle of excitement re-ignites my curiosity.

After Dragon tells me everything I need to know, I rush back into Cain's home and kiss my sleeping twin's forehead in a silent goodbye. I hate leaving her while she's still healing after being poisoned, but I have no choice. Her husband, Silas Whitehart, the Damned Prince, hasn't left her side so I know she's in good hands while I'm gone.

Raven, the harlot who came with them, is waiting in my room when I open the door. There's something about her that I was instantly drawn to the moment I saw her laughing with dried blood on her face while smoking a cigarette. It's been a few days, but we've been inseparable ever since.

She knows about the Trove because her best friend, Silas, works as their healer—the *Druid*, they started calling him. When my sister-in-law, Audrey, was still a harlot, many of them started dying off, and the Trove recruited Raven to be their eyes and ears in the kingdom they believed ran the entire operation. They were right to some extent. Silas' sister was a corrupted madam, and his brother was the muscle behind her, tormenting the poor girls. Raven helped put an end to them.

I tell her all about the meeting with the Trove and Dragon. The second I mention the pleasure house at the bottom of a mountain in the Deimos Kingdom, she smiles wickedly, and for the first time, I realize what others see in me when I know chaos is about to unfold.

Chapter Five

The Deimos Kingdom is known for its mountains and vast, blooming forest that hides its palace away. Even in the winter months, this place isn't touched by snow or the frosty winds. The real Deimos manor isn't far and is rumored to be connected by underground tunnels because the families are so close.

It's taboo, borderline illegal for real and false families to mingle, but the Deimos are the one exception so long as they keep their consorting in private, away from the public eye. None of the other kingdoms would dare risk their safety to do such a thing, except this month, due to the long-awaited wedding that combines two of the most powerful families.

We don't stop in to make our arrival known just yet. It's taken two full nights traveling in the carriage while Raven helped me prepare, and I'm not wasting any time getting started. Raven would say I'm a tad overeager, but I need to see for myself what Dragon thinks I can't handle about Hayse Soren.

"I haven't been here since I was a child." Raven looks nervously out the window. "So much has happened that I hardly remember growing up overseas. And this place…" She blows a raspberry, her head shaking. "I vaguely recall the orphanage being crowded before I was taken to the Whitehart Kingdom." Her sudden high-pitched cackle rattles so loud that I flinch. "Who could say they were thankful to be kidnapped in the middle of the night and dropped off to live with royal harlots?"

"Royal harlots?" I never knew there were varying levels.

She nods. "Royal harlots are trained to stay within the household under the guise of maids, which really means we can fuck as spectacularly as we clean. They didn't let us smoke and I rather hate cleaning so I ran away before I was sold to a family."

The coachman wishes us luck with a knowing wink before we walk through the woods in our silk robes. The path that leads to the stacked boulders at the bottom of the mountain is quick and exactly as Dragon instructed. Funny enough, it's a dragon I imagine sleeping in the dark cave hidden behind the rocks. As we make our way through the black void with Raven's arms looped through mine, I wait to feel the puff of its breath or see the molten fire behind two massive, glowing eyes. I'm so convinced that when the torches flicker in the distance, my heart patters a little faster.

Raven grips my hand with a soft giggle once we see the torches illuminating a decorated drawbridge. Thick chains exit a woman's mouth on either side and disappear into clenched fists. The door itself is carved with naked men and women in precarious positions, giving sultry warnings of what lies behind it.

"Remember?" Raven raises her brow with a soft nudge.

"You're my pet, and my safe word is greenfire. Yours is diablo." I've always considered myself sexually experienced, but I've never needed a safe word before. Raven has taught me things I've never heard of in the last two days, readying me for what I'm about to see and things I may need to do.

Sensing my hesitation, Raven strokes my hair and gives me a tender kiss, reminding me that there isn't a man or woman alive who wouldn't be lured by my temptation. Her words are all I need to grab that handle and twist with an eager push.

A wave of pure terror and excitement floods me. The scent of sweet tobacco, spiced wine, leather, and velvet hit me all at once. As my nose works through the exotic mix, my ears pick up the sultry moans, heated whispers, sharp slapping of skin, and words slipped in the heat of pleasure. It's the piano in the corner that has my lips tugging a little higher. A lullaby of lust-laced poetry wraps around me.

"Fuck me," Raven's deep blue eyes widen with a smile spreading across her cheeky face. Her chestnut hair sits at her shoulders, drawing attention to the golden collar around her neck. "This is why I remained a harlot." She squeals at my side, tugging at my arm. I swear her energy is spreading through her skin and into mine because I sure as shit can't lower my grin, either. "I know I'm your pet, but I can't wait to head for the spanking benches. I love making a *bad boy* squirm."

"Rav—" Her heated glare stops me.

Holy Hell, this girl has me thinking we should have switched roles. I thought being in the pet role would make me weak, and my inability to hold my tongue would give us away, but with the soft amber light shadowing the cragged walls and cerulean curtains, the sacrilege sounds with bodies snaking along the round chaises... I'd let her spank me in front of all of them.

"*Pet*," I quickly correct, spotting the gargoyle-like statues of beautiful men and women scattered around the cavernous room. I notice that half of the people are wearing masks to hide their identities.

Smart—something we obviously aren't.

I swear I was going to ask her a question, but the moment I follow where heads turn and see *him*, I'm transfixed. It's the way he sits alone on the round chaise wearing only black pants, one leg kicked out and the other lifted with his hand resting on his knee without a care. His other hand rests on his lower stomach that is covered in black ink. A burning swig hangs from his lips as he watches a couple fucking on the chaise next to him. It isn't his white hair that gives him away, but the self-assured, cocky aura exuding from his relaxed posture, warning others away— *Hayse Soren*.

The metal through his nipples is what draws me in. It's frightening to witness someone possess such chilling, brutal beauty. To be able to hold the breath of everyone in the room. If he told us all to fall over and die, I'm not sure who would be left. This man is the most dangerous man I've ever laid eyes on.

Dragon was right, he isn't like other men. He's a god.

The feral side I keep bound with crafted medicinal powders slithers out of her cage at the challenge.

"Oh, spank me with a spike." Raven leans into my ear. "I would let him do *any single thing* he wanted to do to me. I'd forget my safe word and—"

"He's arrogant," I cut her off and pull her toward the corner by her leash. "He thinks he owns the room because he's pretty." I open the onyx ring on my finger, dip my pinky nail into the *serenade snuff* I created, and take it in through my nose. It's not what others take that gives them a rush, but my own concoction that calms me down when I start to get too overstimulated, allowing me a better chance at holding my tongue. I can't afford to cause a scene right now, and that feral fiend within me is surely to take over if I don't smother her back down.

Raven sheds her robe, the blue lace shimmering against her golden skin, plumping her breasts closer to her neck. I consider myself fortunate to have a large chest, but Raven was blessed with a bust that has every head turning toward us. She knows it, too. She gives me a wink and offers to get us a drink. While any other time I would have already been at the bar and drunk a bottle empty, I need my head straight.

The serenade snuff has already kicked in. My heart rate has slowed with a wave of calm passing over me.

Gripping Raven's leash, I wink back at her, hold my head high, and walk straight toward Hayse. My heels clack with every step while Raven's soft feet patter behind me at a steady pace. Heads continue to turn, but I'm used to unwanted attention and don't bother giving them any of mine as I continue toward my target.

My stomach drops to my elevated toes as we stop before him. He either doesn't see us approach or is so into the scene next to him that he doesn't notice.

I clear my throat.

A puff of smoke rises as he drags his head toward us, stopping at Raven, who lets out a low squeal.

He doesn't say a word, doesn't smile or show any interest other than a quick jerk of his head, beckoning her to him.

Low gasps sound around the room. The piano key falters before finding its rhythm again.

He doesn't invite anyone onto his chaise, that's what Dragon said. He enjoys watching or commanding others. The rare few he's invited to his backroom said he was too much but never explained why.

My hand tightens on Raven's leash as she steps forward, circling it around my hand again and again until it's so tight, she's at my side with her head angled to my shoulder.

"If you're not going to let her play, what do you want?" His voice is rich and harsh. It's hard not to get distracted by the white birthmark running down the center of his chest or the glistening piercings. What's even worse are his eyes. Solid black, soulless voids that I want to burn in. Not a god then, but the damn Devil himself.

"I wanted to see what all the fuss was about." I curl my lip. "How… *disappointing*."

My shoes squeal as I turn on my heel, making a point to drag Raven toward the spanking benches so she can have her fun.

I made my statement, and while we wait for his response, I'm going to need Raven to help release the overflowing energy that's built inside me the moment I saw him.

"Stop." Hayse's harsh voice almost has me jerking at the command, but I'd rather sit on broken glass than let him think he can order me around that easily. I keep my even pace as if I didn't hear him, ensuring the points in my heels are loud and clear.

A girl steps in my path, her eyes wide with bewilderment as she grasps my shoulders. "*Hayse* is calling you."

"I know." I toss my platinum hair over my shoulder. "I'm not interested."

"But…" She leans into my ear. "No one gets a chance with Hayse. It's…" She struggles to find the words. "*Please*. We've all waited to see him."

I tilt my head back, finding Hayse on the edge of his chaise, watching and waiting to see what I'll do. My father's voice rings in my ear about never doing a favor for anyone without getting something in return. "Buy me a bottle of the best bubbly and red, and I'll put on my best show for you."

The girl grabs my face and kisses my cheek, showering me with overjoyed thanks before skipping to the bar. The barkeep's mouth gapes as she talks to him, eyeing the distance between me and the Devil behind me. I notice the familiar dragon mask amongst the room of onlookers as I turn back. "Did you say something?"

His attention remains on my pet. "Crawl."

Raven doesn't hesitate to lower to her knees, pausing when he holds his hand in silent command to stop before she makes it all the way. "Not you." His lips twitch, giving away his amusement. "Put the collar on your master and order her to crawl to me."

Part of me wants to play into whatever this is, but the real me can't hide from smug bastards like him, no matter how much serenade snuff I ingest. With one quick motion, I unsnap Raven's collar and nod her toward the spanking benches. "Go play, pet."

Raven gives me a knowing grin before sauntering off. "She's busy."

"You don't like doing what you're told, do you?"

"That's funny," I examine my nails. "I didn't hear you tell *me* to do anything. Did anyone else?" I toss my head to the side, where I'm met with a mix of nods, shakes, and unassumed gazes that lift to the ceiling. Dragon's shoulders shake in the corner.

Hayse's stony face falls with a glower that would send me to my grave if I weren't already the Devil's Doll, the Wicked Witch, or Satan's Spawn. "If you want to play, *kneel* and crawl to me." He accentuates *kneel* like he's a king commanding a peasant to show him respect.

Every head in the room turns to me. Doors click open down a hall, and more people fill what felt like a massive room moments ago.

"Say, please." I shed my thin robe, dropping it to my feet. I'm in a black lacy bra and underwear that hikes so far up my ass I don't know why I wore them. Most of these people are naked or in similar outfits, but it's all in the attitude. He could look to his right and find a woman with bigger tits or look to his left and continue watching a gorgeous, luscious woman ride a man with more enthusiasm than I've ever shown during sex.

But his murderous eyes remain on *me*.

I don't realize I'm holding my breath until I watch the subtle change in his demeanor. The scowl he's been giving me shifts to a placated mask that's almost charming if it were on someone who could possess such a trait. The way his lips widen is fake, and his voice rises an octave that gives way to something I can't place yet. "Please give the people what they want and crawl to me, *wicked* one."

My belly dips as if it were made of hot honey.

A promise is a promise. I turn my head to the woman with my free wine, finding an anxious lust on her pretty face as I drop to my knees. The heels make it awkward, but I'm well practiced.

"Do you need me to repeat the instructions, or can you handle the simple task of crawling without being reminded?"

I hate this man. My body burns with a fire that's usually a constant flicker deep in my belly but is now roaring through my flushed skin.

Keeping my eyes locked on his, I crawl, my hands and legs slowly dragging in sync.

Regardless of the man it's for, this is what I love—the seduction. I sway my hips and arch my back for those behind me. I lick my lips and push my chest together for those in front of me.

I've never been watched in front of a group before, but I can proudly say that it's one of the hottest things I've ever experienced, knowing they're all looking at *me*, desiring *me*, *envying* me.

Hayse stands, taking the four steps to bridge the gap between us before crouching to my level. With a single finger, he lifts my chin. An amethyst ring sparkling on his finger catches my eye.

"You like being told what to do, don't you? Even though you fight against it." My legs clench to stop the throbbing that starts at the apex of my thighs. "But do you really think I'd let you touch me?"

His condescending laugh sends a spike of adrenaline straight through spine. He tosses my chin, and as he stands to leave, I'm left with a fury that has my mouth acting before I can think.

A dark cackle leaves my throat. "It's a shame someone so desirable is so boring." I look him up and down as I lift to my heels. "I'm not the slightest bit surprised. All pretty boys are empty and useless."

Walking past him, I contain the petty urge to shove his shoulder with mine when I find a man on a velvet sofa, licking his lips at me.

With a devious idea, I sway my hips the way I did on the floor with a sultry smile that he can't deny is for him. "Need a hand, handsome?"

If Hayse prefers watching, I'll give him a show that will make him regret turning me away. Bastard.

The man's throat bobs as I lower to the chaise, my knees falling between his legs. I start to crawl over him when my hair is pulled back, arching my neck to its limit until I'm met with those black, beady voids. "What do you think you're doing?" A husky growl leaves Hayse's throat.

I reach for the man to show him exactly what I was about to do, my fingers grazing his shaft. Hayse loops my arms by the elbows in one movement and drags me off him. He doesn't stop, forcing me to stumble, bumbling against his side through the main room. "Get back on the floor."

"No."

"You're a brat," he snarls tightly against my ear. "Unlucky for you, I enjoy taming brats." He pulls my hair harder, yanking my head back once again to see the seriousness in his beautiful face. "Get. On. The. Fucking. Floor. Or say your safe word and leave."

I swallow my argument. I have no other choice. I'm not going to quit and lose my chance at the Trove, no matter how much I want to do the opposite of everything this man says.

"I can't get on the floor when you're holding me against you." At his bitter realization, he releases me.

I drop to my knees, my mind working too slow to understand the bench before me until it's too late. Hayse steps around it and secures my wrist to one end. The panic sets in and I hurry to hide my other wrist behind my back before he can tie it down too.

"You're my favorite, Amelvira. Why do you make me do this to you?" My father's voice echoes through my head.

Hayse doesn't say anything. He simply holds his hand out with a raised brow and a look that says he's counting to three before he takes what he wants.

My throat dries. I *have* to do this.

Sealing my eyes tight, I place my shaking hand into his, wincing when he secures it tighter than the first one. I thank every divine deity that I can think of that I ingested the serenade snuff before this. The screams rattling in my head would bring this mountain down.

"I don't like hurting you, but you need to learn to behave, Rosebud."

Hands are on my cheeks, prying my eyes open until I release them and find Hayse studying me with a triumphant look I turn from. "Not a fan of ties?" I swallow the lump in the back of my throat, feeling his thumb spreading a tear I didn't know had fallen to the side of my cheeks. "What's your safe word?"

"Greenfire," I say without hesitating. It's on the tip of my tongue to repeat it to get out of these restraints, but I can't lose this moment.

"Good. I sincerely hope you don't use it." He stands, and I see the golden cane he's holding between his hands, the shimmering green handle in his palm, before he disappears behind me.

My pulse rises. The rapid beating of my heart pounds in my ears. A gentle tap of cold metal on my backside makes me hiss.

I find Raven standing in the distance, her mouth parted with a heated look and a smirk slowly lifting up her cheeks. "Bad girl," she mouths.

Smack!

I was about to laugh when a sharp sting has me crying out. "Approaching me without an invitation." Another sharp *smack*, lower on my ass, has me biting my lip. "Not listening when I call you to me." Again and again, the cane *cracks* down harder on me, pulling out deeper whimpers and gasps I can't hold back. The burn on my cheeks is nothing compared to the heat boiling through my blood and center. The throbbing…

His hands are in my hair again, pulling my head up to meet his. "You take your punishments well." He lowers behind me, his lips grazing my ear. "Say, thank you."

"Fuck you." I have enough room in my restraints to turn my wrists and give him both my middle fingers with a smile.

His lips lift to one side before he leans into my ear again. "I'm going to have so much fun breaking you, *Amelvira, Lunasol, Aramos.*"

My heart stills in my chest as the world closes in around me. He shouldn't know who I am. I'm a princess, a *real* princess. Our identities are hidden. To the rest of the world that isn't royal, I'm just Mel, an unassuming girl from 'another town,' no matter where we go.

My shock must be written on my face because he pulls away with a winning grin.

"Untie her," a familiar voice comes from behind me that the crowd disperses for. When he crouches in front of me, he holds my face in his warm hands, and his big, brown eyes soften. "Mi Vera, what are you doing here?"

Me?

I look around but don't see any sign of Hayse as Percival works to untie my wrists and lifts me in his arms, carrying me to a backroom, where he lays me on a bed and rubs a warm salve on my burning welts.

"The wedding, of course," I finally answer, wincing every now and again at the tender sting.

"That's not what I meant." Percival huffs with a familiar annoyance. "What are you doing in the Forbidden Den?"

"*Hmm...* Shouldn't I be asking you the same question?" I let loose a tired giggle and hear his softly joining mine. "I was just having a little fun before the wedding is officially public, *husband*."

Darling Devil

My Devil Doll is so pretty when she's crying. I never thought I'd see the day when tears ran down Amelvira's sharp cheeks, but today is a joyous day indeed.

The welts on her looked painful. As always, she's too proud and perfect, attempting to bite her lip to keep from wailing those sultry grunts, but in the end, she blessed us all with her sinful song. I wasn't the only one captivated by her; the entire den couldn't look away.

I've *never* been able to look away.

It's been sixteen years of latching onto any glimpses I could, and it's not just because of her lethal beauty; it's the mayhem that ensues everywhere she goes. She's an addictive experience. A vice I crave and can't quit.

I can't wait to see how close she's willing to get, how far she's willing to go, to achieve the task the Trove gave her. I have no doubt she'll succeed, but what she doesn't know is that she won't get the chance to join them.

I already have our ending mapped out perfectly. Mel's always had an infatuation with all witchcraft, chaos, and hellish things, absorbing, becoming, and using what people throw at her as her own virtuous shield, and I'm more than willing to give her what she wants.

The endearing term, Devil Doll, really is perfect for her because her life is about to become the Hell she craves, with me as her darling Devil and her as my little doll, strung like a marionette in the scenes I orchestrate.

And by the end, it will only be us.

Chapter Six

Now

"You're alive!" Percival rushes toward me, pulling me into a tight embrace before holding me at arm's length to look me over. "Only you can make barbaric scars stunning." His brown waves shake as his head does, and a genuine smile creeps up the taut angles of his face. Stubble graces his strong jaw, and there's a heaviness in his warm eyes that says the last few days have been too much. "Raven and Blair are safe at an inn near town. I told them to stay put while I searched for you two."

A weight physically lifts off my chest knowing Raven is okay. When I asked Hayse, he shrugged and said, "Your pet will be fine." Knowing Blair is safe too is a relief. The girl is worse than a lost puppy, but I have to admit I'd contemplate shedding a tear if she were harmed. Not so much her aunts.

Hayse leans against the door, arms crossed, as he watches us with a blank expression. Seeing me notice him, his grin twitches. Lifting his fingers between his lips, he slowly drags them out until they release with a silent pop.

"What's wrong? Did I hurt you?" Percival reacts to my sharp inhale.

"I um… no, I just realized I should go pick more berries. You must be starving." I grab the basket by the door, toss the burnt-out cigarette at Hayse, and shove him to the side, leaving before either of them can take me any more by surprise.

I favor rain over sun, but I'll take any excuse to trick myself that it's the bright rays overheating my body as I close the door behind me.

Flopping onto the grass, I cross my legs and start pulling at the blackberries and blueberries overtaking the small cottage, wishing it was night so the full moon could cleanse and recharge me. As I work, I contemplate what could have led me here based on the memories I'm able to recall. It's not much to go on.

Percival didn't seem surprised or worried to find me here with Hayse, which means we all must be close, right? I've always been close to Percival, but Hayse? I don't see myself becoming *friends* with him. But then, how do *they* know each other? Is it from the Den?

The mountain in the near distance is the same one that the Forbidden Den is tucked within. Probably a day's walk away. I look back at it, the peak jutting over the tops of the trees. I recall Raven telling me that the Forbidden Den was thought to be a hellish lair full of witches before it became a place for carnal debauchery.

Must be your relatives. I can hear Hayse's mocking jest already.

By the time I fill the basket and open the door, ready to face my demons, hushed angry whispers greet me first. "I wanted them all to go to sleep, not fucking die! Someone messed with—" The squealing door cuts off Hayse's voice. Both men are flushed in the face, their attention turned toward me.

I slam the door with my foot. "Who died?"

Hours later, Raven jumps into my arms, her legs wrapping around my waist as we fall onto the couch. She looks awful. Her hair is frizzy, her eye has a yellow tint from a healing bruise, while her clothes are ragged, smelling of sweat and the woodsy air. Blair is a similar mess, standing shyly by the door, except her sun-glowing hair is tied at the nape of her neck, and she doesn't sport any bruises.

"Percival and Blair were being taken by the guards, but I stepped in, using my assets to save them." Raven gives me a proud wink, swiveling her sights to where Percival snickers while grazing on berries. "It took him a minute to see the diversion I created. And now we're all wanted. They think we all had something to do with the explosion." She snaps her focus on Hayse. "What happened?"

Hayse, as usual, gives a weak shrug and takes out his bag of vices to roll a cigarette. "It was a wedding. Explosions went off. I found Mel and brought us here to hide."

"He won't tell me anything either," I huff at Raven, who doesn't look convinced as I continue telling them all the last thing I remember.

"That was a month ago, Mel. You're telling me you don't remember anything after the first time in the Den?"

"Maybe we could reenact things that happened," Blair suggests, walking toward the fireplace. "They say smells or certain sights can trigger memories. Do you have wine?"

"We want to trigger the last month, not the last twenty years of her life." Percival winks at me.

"When you first arrived at the palace, you…" Blair's cheeks redden.

"I, what?"

Hayse lets out a dark chuckle as smoke leaves his mouth, his long fingers pulling the paper from his tilted lips. "You were a fucking nightmare."

"How would *you* know?" My eyes pierce straight through him.

"You really don't remember who I am, do you?"

CRUEL KINGDOMS

Blair tosses a log and lit match into the fireplace. The burst of flame brings forth vivid memories that seem too distant. The scars on my skin are shallow compared to the ones that burst deep within my chest.

Chapter Seven

One Month Ago

My husband, Percival Deimos, is the prince and heir of King Hale Deimos, whose kingdom's words are: *Golden and graceful, with lips so sweet you won't taste the sin 'til you sleep.* Their playhouses and wine groves are what they're best known for, though their vineyards aren't whispered in mythical whispers like the Forbidden Den is. I wasn't entirely sure it was real until yesterday, and I still wouldn't believe it if my backside weren't aching and throbbing, increasing violently with every sharp clack of my heels.

False royals are grandiose, and then there is Hale Deimos' double, the Deimos false king. I've been in this palace once before, and nothing has compared since, yet as I walk down the west wing, I'm taken aback at just how brassy this king is. It's impressive.

One would think a rolling royal garden would be sufficient, but the man put a glass conservatory and menagerie in the center of the property.

He doesn't attend church, he owns one. The gaudy cathedral is the most beautiful thing about this place. The only building that isn't draped in ivory and gold but smokey gray, onyx, and stained-glass windows depicting religious sigils. I'm sure if I step foot in there, I'll burn, so I'll take to admiring it from afar.

The Trove's task isn't the only reason that I find myself in the Deimos' opulent kingdom. After my father burned their vineyards to ash during one of his *episodes*, they retaliated by burning our loom houses, silk gardens, wardrobe vaults, and spinning wheels. Their hatred for one another had gone too far that time, forcing my father to do the one thing he would never do: bow.

I was eight when we came here. It was the first and only time I ever saw a sliver of fear in the powerful man as he ordered me to charm Percival and gather whatever secrets I could while he met with the kings.

Needless to say, I succeeded. With a few high-pitch giggles and suggestive hand grazes, Percival told me all about the secret playhouses and overseas connections dealing with exotic animals. My father used that knowledge to leverage an alliance.

I've been chasing the high of making him that proud ever since.

What I didn't know at the time was that I signed away my freedom that day. The forced alliance was held together by the binding marriage contract between Percival and me.

Technically, we've been married for sixteen years, but the kings all agreed to wait to make it public so they could dangle us as options to other kingdoms to help forge whatever deals they must.

Percival, although our visits are infrequent, has been my sanctum ever since.

We didn't sleep together until years later. He was my first, someone I turned to when my sister, Eva, was kidnapped. Someone I still turn to when the opportunity presents itself. He loves sneaking into the false balls just as much as I do.

We're similar in most ways. Our yearning for freedom led us to a pact that allows us to be with whoever we want until our marriage is public. Finding me in the Den might have been a surprise, but nothing outside of our agreement.

"I can't believe you're married!" Raven rasps quietly as we make our way toward the great hall. Even the corridors are horrifically glittery with ornamental candelabras and flashy relics in glass cases. Rich paintings line every turn with tasseled runners disgraced by my stabbing heels.

I *tsk* to myself. False royals love to flaunt the wealth we earn for them as if they're entitled to it. They are to some degree. While they control the battle of the public, we're in the background doing the real work.

"Technically speaking." I grab two flutes of champagne off a passing serving tray and take them back, abandoning the glasses in a nearby plant. "If you're interested, you have a month until we're both officially monogamous. He'll bend you every which way you couldn't possibly imagine."

Her eyes glitter with an ocean's promising storm. "Will he let me bend him?"

My simpering smirk has her walking a little lighter, her glances darting around to lay her sights on the man who is going to fall head over heels for her. If there's anything Percival likes, it's a confident woman who doesn't deny herself what she wants.

The monogamy is something we might have to discuss after the wedding. It's not that I want to be with other people, I just know my father won't stop using me to get what he needs, husband or not. Royalty is coveted, something people pay an astronomical amount to experience with blood, money, and deals.

You're welcome, Blair. I spot my false double the moment we enter the great hall; her glowing golden hair falls to her elbows, and I swear I see a halo around her forehead where baby cherubs are holding it over her precious diadem. Her blush dress is modest and makes her look like a delicate cupcake.

Being that this is the one kingdom my father secured when I was still young, it's the one kingdom I don't know much about. All the others, my father forced me to learn thoroughly to understand my target enough to seduce what I needed out of them.

I know of Blair Somberlain because when I sneak into the false balls, she follows me around like a stray kitten, asking me questions about myself so she can be the best double there ever was. She's cute, bubbly, and loved, whereas I'm a 'temptress,' chaotic, and loathed. Classic little princess and wicked witch tale.

"Who did you piss off?" Raven asks, noticing the sneers and wide berth others give us as we stroll around in search of wine. I can see her head jerking to all the lavish details, the marbled columns, the chandeliers dripped with rubies and sapphires, the emeralds embedded in chalices, the abundance of woven tapestries, the many turning heads with red-stained lips hidden behind cupped whispers.

A soft understanding settles over her as to why I dressed us both in my finest silks. Hers is an off-the-shoulder, navy, princess-cut dress with a skirt that subtly widens her hips. There was no hiding her cleavage, so I decorated the swells of her breasts with a citrine necklace that brightens her blue eyes. Mine matches in every way except my dress is a shimmering black, my necklace is a purple garnet, and my heels are three inches higher—the witchy glamour everyone expects of me.

"For starters, everyone." I smirk and wave at a woman I'm positive I threw a snake at last year for calling me one, and another I once bedded, where I learned her brother has a nasty thievery habit. There is certain to be a few candelabras or necklaces missing by the end of the night if he's in attendance.

Grabbing two more flutes, I'm ready to show Raven how to appropriately disappear into the wall and watch everyone from afar, when I see the last person I expected to be here, standing with Blair and her three horrid aunts. "What is *he* doing here?"

Right now would be the perfect time to find a corner and ingest my serenade snuff, but I'm too focused on the wide smile Hayse is giving

Blair's aunts while the princess's eyes dazzle up at him, worshiping his every word.

There's no hatred glower or crease between his brow, no tight fists, or cigarettes. *No cane.* With a red and black fitted suit and his white slicked-back hair, he looks like all the men I've ever hated wrapped into a perfect tempting gift.

His head tilts back, the bulge in his throat bobs as he laughs again, waving off Blair's offered glass. *Fake.*

I despise liars, and as I watch him closer, I see the perfect mask he wears that hides the sadist I was introduced to last night.

I prefer the malevolent devil.

Raven takes one of my flutes, finishes it, and threads her arm through mine. "Let's go find out."

I might have to ask Percival how he feels about adopting an adult because I can't think of another way to keep Raven by my side for the rest of my life besides outright marrying her to us. She said she'd never marry but I won't let her or Percival object to me keeping her.

As we near, inconspicuously taking in a tapestry that depicts this very palace at sunset, I catch a piece of their conversation that makes me want to vomit into my glass. I keep a tight hold on the empty flute in case I do just that.

"She's always been a beauty, even as a baby. I swear, she was like a perfect little flower," Fern, the aunt who favors red silks, gushes about Blair. She is my least favorite of the three. Her voice never rises above a calm conversation, but a single glance can make a giant feel like a tiny, songless bird.

Florence, the one in green, is the whimsical one of the bunch and the one I don't mind. Her eyes are wide, and her voice is soft, with words that tumble out, always cut too short when the other two nudge her to stop. "Oh yes, Blair's voice is spectacular, too. You must hear her sing, it's like… it's like… well, it's beautiful, really."

Margarette, the plump one who looks like a giant blueberry, is the one to nudge her before she continues rambling.

Thank the divine. If I have to hear them say another—

"She's even magnificent when she sleeps," the plump aunt adds.

Maybe she should stay that way. The five of them turn toward me. *Shit.* I might have said that out loud.

"What did you say?" Fern cuts her famous glare toward me. It's Hayse my attention falls on, if only to get away from the sinking feeling in my gut at the woman's motherly disappointment.

His smile isn't wide, but it tilts to the side, genuinely amused by the ordeal I found myself in. What's worse is the way it falls into a penetrating scowl as he takes in my ensemble, giving a glimpse of the vindictive fiend within. He looks like he wants to bend me over and take the cane to me again.

I may threaten Cain enough to despise me, but I surely haven't actually pissed in Hayse's oats so what the hell is this man's problem with me?

"It's a rhetorical question," Margarette sneers. "We heard what you said, you wretched—"

"Now, now," Fern places her hand on Margarette's shoulder to calm her. "We don't stoop to her level with name-calling, and while I would normally suggest we show her love and kindness, she knows nothing of such basic tact. Not even our empathy would be useful on her because she doesn't understand the concept. Why, I'm sure helping others would give her a heart attack." Her smile lifts with the evil she claims I possess. Her words mean nothing to me and aren't anything I haven't heard over the years. "She's just another soulless Aramos with an unholy soul, just like her demented twin."

Boiling fury rushes straight to my head. It's too late to sniff the medicinal powder in my ring, and the striking serpent inside me is too much to hold back. Why did she have to bring Eva into this?

"You're right." I take a step so we're a breath apart. "I do know nothing of love and kindness, which means, if I were three peasants who just insulted a princess known as Satan's Spawn, I'd make sure my doors were locked nice and tight tonight."

Lifting the flute from her hand, I toss the empty one over my shoulder, hearing it shatter somewhere behind me. I could step back and give us room, but this is so much more fun. Bringing the champagne to my lips, the bottom nips the end of her nose as I finish my fifth glass.

"And save your apologies, not only would they insult me further, but it might piss me off enough to do something more permanent." Fern's head jerks as I twirl my fingers through her graying hair. "Women like you value beauty and a pretty voice, right? Pretty flowers?"

I glance at Blair, who's looking at me like I'm her savior. I'm aware she worships me, but I just threatened her and her aunts. Her naivety goes beyond appearances, then, which is truly astonishing.

Poor thing.

As I take in the purple in her eyes, I'm reminded how serious she is about playing my double. The contacts she wears don't have the mix of hazel and violet that resembles the golden dawn like mine. Her hair has lightened over the years as well, but while she tries in appearances, her entire façade is nothing close to me. I've heard about her going to town to grace the common folk with her gracious smile and beautiful songs, something I would never do. Call me wretched all you want, but I'm not fake, unless I'm messing with someone who deserves it.

Shoving the empty glass to Margarette, I turn and leave, but not before giving Blair a wink to piss them off.

The only other thing I know about the princess is that the false King Deimos took a liking to her once our marriage was confirmed within the need-to-know circle. After Blair's parents tragically died of a plague they caught while visiting the Whitehart Kingdom years ago, the false King Deimos took Blair in and treated her as his own. Her siblings, Cain and Eva's doubles, were under the care of their aunts until they married off, but they've always doted on Blair just as my own father favored me.

My father did have his double replaced for appearance's sake, but I don't blame Blair and the rest of her family for not living with the stranger.

It's all a shitshow, in my opinion. A bunch of scared men who shield themselves behind those they believe are lesser than them to ease the pressure they can't handle.

"Have I told you I love you yet?" Raven snickers beside me. "Your threats—"

"They aren't threats," I assure her.

Dinner is announced, and we take our seats. With Raven on my left, Percival is on my right. His father, King Hale Deimos, is on his other side, offering me a curt nod in greeting, his second chin hitting the top of his chest. He's much older than the other kings, his graying hair giving away his age, but the weight he holds makes him appear younger in the face. He's not my biggest fan since it's my fault he's aligned with my family.

I look down the line, eager to see who Blair has the fortune or misfortune of being tied to for the rest of her life. For her sake, I hope he's kind. Her softness is too childish for court and will get her hurt if she doesn't have someone both kind and strong.

But that's not the case.

All the air is sucked from my lungs for a second time tonight when I see who takes the seat between the false king and Blair—*Hayse*.

MALICIOUS INTENTIONS

He doesn't look like the false King Deimos, who has shaggy black hair and a matching black beard. His beady eyes aren't as hateful either, though they do hold a certain sternness that most kings do.

Dragon failed to mention that the task he gave me is suicidal. If Hayse Soren is the false prince, my husband's double, I might as well sign my death certificate now. While the Deimos are known for their close relationship with their doubles, *consorting* with them sexually is illegal—something I've dabbled in, but not with someone so public. This is *his* royal wedding. All eyes will be on him this month.

My throat dries. Everyone around me becomes intensely familiar. Half of the room I've slept with, the other half I've scared off. As much as I loathe doing my father's dirty work, seducing others for secrets, I've found a way to make peace with it. And while I've always thought I held power over them, I feel like I'm on display—a witch about to be burned at the stake.

I'm cursing myself for not knowing about Hayse. I would have noticed *him* at the false balls, but I supposed there was no reason for him to attend with the arranged marriage in place. Still, Blair always went.

As the plates and courses are passed around, I wait patiently until it's evident none are being placed in front of me on purpose.

Raven bumps me with a curious look, but I tell her not to worry as I tap my glass, signaling Oliver, the minstrel, to refill it to the brim. Others take note that I'm not being served and snicker in my direction.

"I'm allergic to fish," I say loud enough for the gossip to be that I refused dinner rather than someone trying to play a childish prank on me.

Leaning into Raven, I quickly introduce her to Percival and tell her to stay and enjoy herself while I excuse myself from the mind-numbing feast. With the kings' booming laughter and voices overpowering most of the other conversations, no one hears me, and I'm able to take my leave without notice.

I already know what's to come, speech after speech, adoring Blair, and how happy everyone is that she and Hayse will be joined after such a long wait. This feast is for them, so my absence won't be missed, or at least cared about.

Taking a candle from a nearby candelabra, I ask Oliver, who is hurrying down the hall with more wine, where I might find Blair's aunt's chambers. He gives me a mischievous grin and points me in the direction, only after I promise to find him later so we can sneak a few bottles of the old vintage merlot while he plays his lute or guitar.

He's my favorite to seek out at the false balls. His lips are looser than a whore's—I stop myself mid-thought. It's a habit to speak so shamelessly, one I'm trying to rid myself of since learning my sister-in-law, Audrey, used to be a harlot. I'm making a conscious effort not to say degrading things unless it's to hurt someone's feelings.

As a thank you, I pass Oliver a velvet bag of the pixie powder that he loves. I'm more selective about who I share my concoctions with after I mistakenly trusted another princess, Aspen, with a love drug that was used on my sister. Knowing my father would exploit my craft, I keep it under wraps the best I can.

I'm five minutes into my walk, entering the west wing, when my ears pick up soft footsteps behind me.

When I turn, there's no one there.

I start again, this time turning my head back as I continue clacking my heels. A small girl gasps when she sees me notice her, jumping into a hidden alcove in the wall.

"Come out." My voice is harsher than I mean.

"I'm s-s-sorry," she stutters. Her eyes are on her feet as she shuffles from the wall.

"Don't be sorry." I lift her chin, biting my shock at the scars along her cheeks and flash of scales that were too deep to cut away: *The Mark of the*

Beast, or *Hell's Harsh Kiss* depending on the myth one believes. Leaning to her level, I brush my thumb along the rough skin. "What is it you want, beautiful?"

Her cheeks redden, her hands wringing her tiny apron. She must be one of the servant children. "Y-y-you don't have to call me that. I-I'm nothing like you. I j-just wanted to see one up close."

My brows knit tightly.

"A witch," she adds shyly.

I give her a cackle that makes her brows rise. "Are you scared?"

"No." Her head shakes furiously. "You're so pretty. I w-wish I looked like you."

This girl is too sweet. She must be around seven, the same age when the wickedness seeped into me. Taking her black hair between my fingers, I tuck it behind her ear. "Looks fade, darling. My hair will gray, my skin will wrinkle, but it's the reputation that will remain." I give her a wink. "The witch will outlive us both, I'm afraid."

A coy smile graces her cheeks. "They say h-horrible things about you."

I shrug and straighten my legs, holding the candle between us. "Words are for the weak. Are you weak?"

Her mouth opens and closes, trying to figure out her entire life path at this moment.

"You aren't," I tell her with all the confidence I have. "You could have stayed back like the rest of them, but you chased the wicked witch down the hall just to get a peek. Remember that."

She nods her head, unconvinced, and disappears through another small alcove hidden within the wall. Something reckless stirs inside of me, a need to prove myself outside of my beauty for this child to see it's all smoke and mirrors to hide my scaling serpent slithering beneath the surface.

It doesn't take too much longer to find Fern's chambers, *unlocked*. The flowery perfumes take me to the lavish balcony where her perfect garden resides. It's so neat and orderly, so well-manicured. It's a shame there's no light out here to take it all in.

I stick the candle in the center, using the point of my nail to push it over.

Oops.

The flames lap up each petal quickly.

My stomach tickles by the time I leave, practically skipping to meet Oliver in the wine cellar when I see white hair disappear down the hallway.

I suppose it's time to see what secrets Hayse is hiding.

Darling Devil

Humiliating the vicious Devil Doll didn't go as planned. I expected her to make a scene about not being served, but all she did was take it in stride before stalking off from the feast entirely.

The Somberlain sisters clawed their way under her skin though.

Mel's never been able to hide her genuine emotions. The moment they mentioned her sister, I watched her entire demeanor change in an instant. Rumors about her twin's mental state have circled for years, some saying she's possessed by evil spirits and others whispering that she sees ghosts. I'm positive it's why Mel leans so hard into being sinister, so everyone turns to her and away from Eva, which begs the question, why, if not for cause?

I wonder if she holds the same sentimental attachment to the woman she came with. I have never seen them together before, but I saw the softness in Mel's violet eyes when the brunette spoke to her. They share a similar aura, a confident energy about them that draws other's attention.

It appears I have another doll to play with.

Chapter Eight

The door doesn't close before I shove my foot in the crack and push myself into the room Hayse entered.

He's tossing his black waistcoat and starting to unbutton his red shirt by the time he looks back with a shake of his head. "I'm sure you imagined me in your room, but you're about four doors down from it."

I lean my back against the door, twisting the lock behind me. "And here I thought I was making your dreams come true by being in yours."

While my body is still buzzing from setting the fire to Fern's prized garden, I'm mostly frazzled not to have anything to go on that could help drag out any secrets Hayse may hold about the overseas royals. The Deimos already have alliances with some of them, so Hayse's name as a topic of conversation is logical. But Dragon also said to keep him close in case the Trove can use him, so I have to play nice.

"I assure you," Rather than continue unbuttoning his shirt, he quickly pulls it over his head and folds it with a delicacy I wouldn't bet my tits he possessed. Normal people would ball it up and toss it on the floor or in the bin, but he gently places it on top, running his hands over the front to straighten any creases before facing me again. His features harden into a look I've come to recognize as one he reserves for me, the pinched brows, the beady hate behind his eyes. "Anything with you in it is a nightmare."

MALICIOUS INTENTIONS

A low ache flickers in the depths of my core. I'm starting to believe the myths that circle this place, and all kingdoms for that matter. They say my kingdom, the Aramos Kingdom, possess werewolves and vampires, the Whitehearts house ghosts and necromancers, and the Deimos are filled with fairies and nymphs.

The story I know of nymphs is that they're seductive. They know your deepest desires and face you with them, so while they're using your body, all sanity is gone, and you willingly hand over your soul to be devoured.

And right now, I want nothing more than to suck on his neck while he whispers those spiteful words that unravel my sanity bit by bit. My soul would be damned if I let him get his hands on me.

I have no problem doing what it takes to get information from him, and that might be my problem. He's the challenge I've always dreamed of. Hate is something I'm familiar with, but coming from him feels different; it isn't laced with fear, and that realization is putting my task in the back of my mind, in place of needing to understand this personal loathing he has toward me.

I give a half-shrug, half-nod. "A nightmare's an upgrade from Hell, I suppose."

My eyes fall to his chest where his birthmark glows in the soft, buttery candlelight, starting under his collarbone and continuing down to his navel in the shape of a sword. The amethyst ring on his left hand catches my attention again, feminine compared to the rest of him. Maybe his mother's? I can't recall what happened to her, but I know she's dead.

I take one step, then another as I look around his room to learn something, *anything,* about him. It's neat. Neat is a messy word for what I'm looking at. Hayse is precise and orderly about his things. The books on his dresser are lined by size and color, the ink jars are in a straight row. There's an easel in the corner with canvases and paint in flawless alignment. The obsidian covers on his bed are unblemished by creases.

It's the shackles hanging from a metal bar along the top that catch my attention. The foot of the bed holds the same restraints.

"Do you paint?" I point back toward the canvases and hate myself for asking such an idiotic question. Of course, he does. "I mean, do you paint *willing* subjects?" I grab the restraints at the foot of the bed, trying to regulate my breathing as I do.

"Two separate hobbies." He steps into me, looking down his nose as he yanks my hand away. "Why don't you drop that before you give yourself another panic attack? And while you're at it, you can find your husband in his chambers next door. He'll be able to give you what you can handle."

My spine stiffens. "What I can *handle?*" I let out a petty laugh.

"You mean to tell me you can handle being strapped to my bed, bound and stripped of all control while I use any parts of you however I want?" His finger grazes my collarbone as he lifts the necklace from my skin, quickly dropping it with disinterest.

The hitch in my breath gives me away. A victorious smile slithers up his smug face. "That's what I thought."

Irritation smothers the voice of reason that's telling me to leave. Simply being here was risky enough, but now we're flirting with our own demise and that very revelation has me more determined to see this through, my skin tingling with an elated rush.

Giving him a tight smile, I spin on the top of my heel and fan my skirt out as I sit on the edge of his bed. Looking into the pits of his eyes, I lift my wrists.

His grin vanishes. "What are you trying to prove?"

Great question. My specialty is seducing, not groveling. Pouting like a child, practically begging a man who clearly isn't interested in me, is so far beneath me that I'm not sure how I ended up here. There's something about him that I both despise and desire. He's smug and arrogant, stoic and amused in all the wrong ways. Yet there's that hidden serpent in him that silently calls to mine.

I also need him to want me in order to coax the information Dragon sent me for. Sex has always been transactional for me, so I don't know why this suddenly feels different.

"I've had some time to work on empathy, and I came to the conclusion that it would be a shame if you didn't get a chance with me." I tilt my head and look him over head to toe. "And this whole *I'm-so-desirable-yet-unattainable* bully act was a little hot at first, but it's really getting in your way."

I push to my feet. He's so tall that my neck hurts to look up at him as I pull my corset loose and start for the door. "I'll be in my husband's room if you change your mind. He's not as boring as you've been, and he certainly knows how to *handle* me."

Every step weighs heavily on me. I overplayed my hand, and he showed me all his cards. He not only holds hate in his heart but a wall that not even I can penetrate. I knew getting to him would be difficult, but I detest losing these little battles before the war.

With a new motivation to be free of his overbearing presence, I turn the lock and then the handle, my gut twisting with it.

The door doesn't make it an inch before it slams shut.

I jump back, hitting something hard as fingers press into my neck, keeping me tight against a wall of hard muscle.

"I don't think so, wicked one." His voice rumbles against me. "You're going to see just how *boring* I am."

Hayse drags me back to the bed, lifts me by the waist, and tosses me to the center of the mattress. My thoughts flutter away like scattering birds with my sole focus on him crawling on top of me, taking my arms and dragging them above my head.

It's so fast that my instincts take over before I can stop them. My knee slams against his inner thigh, an inch from where I meant to.

His white hair falls over his face with a groan that shifts into a laugh, cold and malicious as he twists around to hold my ankles still enough to restrain them into the padded shackles.

My eyes slam shut.

"You don't get to say no, Amelvira. You're my daughter. I gave you this body, you'll do what I say with it." The memory of my father's voice flashes before me at the familiar taut pull of my body. *"You're going to lie here and let him finish."*

Those restraints weren't padded like these, so small wins.

A touch on my cheek causes me to flinch. My eyes fly open to find Hayse straddling me between his legs, all his weight on his knees while looking me over with that same pissed-off assessing glower he had in the Forbidden Den. "You're crying again." He says it like he doesn't understand the sentiment.

"I'm a girl." I'm not too proud to belittle my gender in a moment of need. "We cry a lot."

The topic of my emotions is the last thing I need his focus on. He strikes me as the type who would stoop as low as he can just to cut a little deeper. I know because I have that same damning, callous look. The difference is he revels in watching whereas I savor the cutting. I saw it when I went after Fern and Blair.

"I must say." I rattle the chains above my head. "I'm not sure I understand the appeal."

"You will." He doesn't miss a beat. "Remember your safe word, if you can't talk, tap the chain with your finger three times, and when I tell you to breathe, do it."

"Why wouldn't I be able to—" The dagger he pulls from his nightstand halts my questions. The curved blade shimmers in greeting as he places the point against my collarbone, teasing it toward the valley of my breasts, not hard enough to bleed but enough that I gasp, watching the thin, pink, trail scratch down me. "Don't you dare!"

"What are the rules?"

"Hayse! This silk—" His hand comes down hard over my mouth.

"Unless you want us both to be hanged, I suggest you keep the shrill down."

My belly knots at how stupid I am, how impulsive and suicidal coming here really was. Between the knots and the uptick fluttering in my heart, I'm wringing with an excited dread that's dangerous for someone like me.

I squint with silent curses as he drags the dagger straight down, slicing from neckline to navel. I should be worried about how I'm going to leave his chambers with my dress in ribbons, but all I can do is watch as he continues shredding the rich fabric and try not to burn under the intense gaze when his eyes flicker back to mine.

"Rules?"

The words tumble out of my mouth. "Greenfire, tap, breathe."

He leans in, his lips brushing against my neck with a thick whisper, "Good girl."

My belly fills with a warmth I don't expect.

His fingers are cold where he's lifting under the center slit he made down my torso and begins peeling away the black fabric. The dagger's nowhere in sight, but it feels like he's pulling me apart with every inch he exposes.

It's painful in an agonizing, anticipating way that's building the dull ache between my thighs.

When he stops at the scar along my lower belly, I freeze. Every part of me tenses, and he notices, making a point to drag the tips of his finger from one end to the other with a look that says he's enjoying seeing me struggle.

"Piss off the wrong person?"

I laugh without meaning to. "Would you believe me if I told you he said he loved me as he did it?"

His head tilts with indifference. "A man willing to love a wicked thing like you is either a liar or out of his mind insane."

I shrug. "Two things can be true at once."

The corner of his mouth twitches as his hands slide back up my stomach and around my ribs, pushing back the split dress until there's nothing but his palms on me.

With the way he's hovering over me, I don't care that I'm bare or that I can feel my nipple pebble as he looks me over. I'm taking him in right back. The tattoos are closer now, allowing me to make out the dark runes across his chest, not only in color but also in meaning—devotion, patience, and vengeance. There are more shadowing designs along his shoulder and down his arms. The ones across his stomach have a slight offset in color that creates a hidden pentagon.

A flame flares through my center as he takes my nipples between his fingers.

"You're going to regret letting me have control over you."

I suck in a sharp groan as he pinches and pulls. My abs tighten at the sting. My knees bend to close but can't with the restraints around my ankles holding me tightly in place.

"You'll have to work hard. Regret is a woman I've never had the displeasure of meeting."

A deep chuckle leaves his throat as his palm lands next to my arms, still tight against my ears. Lowering his head, he takes my other nipple into his mouth. I squirm beneath him as his teeth graze then latch onto the sensitive bud, pulling it up before letting it drop. "I saw the way you admired my piercings."

His weight shifts, and I can feel the stiff bulge brush against my thigh as he leaves the bed, disappearing into the washroom.

I take the chance to look down at myself. Panic rears its head with too many memories threatening to resurface and suffocate me. If I could reach my ring, I'd ingest a little of the serenade snuff to take the edge off, but the moment Hayse returns, I don't need it. Maybe it's knowing I have an out, that he ensured I knew I had one, that fades away the prickling fear to a wave of anxious readiness.

He straddles my waist again, tearing off a piece of my ruined dress, and places it over my eyes. I jerk my head, not making it easy for him, and he still manages to tie it securely in place.

Black. It's all I see, and while my father ensured neither I nor my siblings fear something as intangible as the dark, I can't help the little trickle of alarm that breaks its way through my psyche.

It's not the darkness causing all my other senses to kick into alert; it's the man on top of me. He's callous and too unpredictable.

Greenfire. I can get out of this whenever I want. The problem is, I've never backed down from anything in my life and short of him trying to stab me in the heart, I don't see myself using it.

"I admire your ability to toss venom back at those who curse your name." His words spread through me like sugar in water over a hot flame. People don't praise me—*ever.* Only my father and his compliments are salt on an open wound.

Hayse tugs my nipples harder, causing my head to dig deeper into the mattress.

"Fuck," his voice deepens. I can hear him swallow as he continues to twist and pull until I swear I'm about to black out from the stinging stimulation. "You're going to want to lie *very* still."

Something thin and cold presses against my breasts, too small to tell what it is. It's gone before it returns, rolling along my rib then brushing against my cheek.

The fucker is teasing me with whatever it is, and the not knowing is building something similar to dread.

Every fiber of my being begs to pull away, to fight just to spite him, but there was a dark warning laced in his voice that tells me if I flinch, he'll revel in doing whatever he's about to do until he makes me scream my safe word if I don't listen.

His tongue flicks over my nipple, pulling it into his mouth. When it vanishes, my body arches without meaning to, greedy to lure him back.

"Breathe in." As he orders me to breathe out, I thank the divines that I'm lying down as a sharp sting slices through me. I cry out, his hand slamming down on my mouth, muffling it until it dies out. My heart pounds in my chest as a wave of heat washes through me.

Sweet-burning Hell. It feels like someone threw a bucket of ice water over my head and somehow left me both burning and wide awake.

He repeats the same quick motion with my other nipple. This time I anticipate what's coming and bite my lip to swallow the pain. The most uncomfortable part is when he lifts the blindfold so I can watch him switch the needle with jewelry that has sharp pointy ends that match his.

The look he's giving me is one of pure fascination as his thumbs swipe just below the piercings. The same soft movement he used when he wiped away my tears. "You did good, pretty girl."

Pounding at the door stops the titillating surge his words do to me.

Hayse isn't as panicked as I am.

My dress is ruined. How am I going to explain being in his room without any clothes?

The last thing I see is a damning grin rising higher on his face before the blindfold is placed back over my eyes. I can feel his weight shift off the bed and the covers pulled from under me before being tossed on top, covering me head to toe.

A soft whimper leaves my throat when the heavy material lands on my nipples. I've never felt this sensitive, both painful and euphoric at the same time. My instinct is to yell out for him, demand he come back and release me so I can hide, but as I hear the twist of the lock and handle, I bite my lip harder than before.

"Have you seen Mel?" Percival's voice is distressed, followed by his father's notable grunt. "There's a fire, and my father's convinced she started it. Blair's aunt is irate and demands that we bring her to apologize."

"Haven't seen her," Hayse answers.

"The damn witch can never behave," King Hale mutters, his heavy steps melting away.

"I'm bored out of my mind," Hayse says. "Want to spar?"

"Are you kidding?" Percival whines.

My very same thoughts!

"After that drag of a feast," my husband continues, "I need more than a fight. Let's go to the Den. Mel's friend is already headed there."

Hayse's snicker is cut off by the door clicking shut.

He can't be serious. This has to be a joke. He can't leave me strapped and naked on his bed. How am I supposed to use my safe word if no one is here to hear it?

Wiggling my hands, my shoulders begin to ache at the uncomfortable position, and every movement has my sore nipples rubbing against the heavy covers.

The door clicks again. "Hayse, this isn't funny." His fingers graze my shin. "Hayse, let me out!"

My breath catches as his fingers trail higher on my thighs until he finds my wet center.

"I just had to check." His dark chuckle fills me with even more dread. "Have nightmares about me while I'm gone, wicked one."

Darling Devil

As Mel remains tied under the covers, all I can wonder is if she knows she talks in her sleep. If she did, I'm sure she wouldn't have let herself pass over to the night in a room that isn't hers.

I run my hands over her legs as she grumbles, "Hayse, stop," before begging her father to let her go. She mutters something about overseas and a dragon.

It's risky, but I lower the covers over her head and run my hand through her light hair. "Percival…" She giggles.

There hasn't been a day since the moment I saw her that I haven't wanted to do that.

As I lean over, I can smell the merlot and blackberries on her breath. She has favored the fruit since the day someone struck her with them at one of the balls. Rather than cause a scene, she picked them off the ground, winked, and said thank you because she was famished.

That's what she does. She takes everything thrown at her and makes it her own. Softly, I lower the covers to expose the new jewelry. Her pink-dusted nipples are swollen with the steel spikes stabbed through them.

They suit her so well. Pretty and painful. Something to look at but to dare touch would be a mistake.

I cover her back up. As much as I want to stay, I came for a reason. Taking the tiny sack I brought with me, I reach for her hands, unlatch the ring, and watch the white powder float into it.

I prefer her untamed, and I have better use of the potent snuff.

Raven stands in the corner of the Forbidden Den with a paddle in one hand, laughing maniacally with a man bent over the bench. Mel couldn't have found someone who matches her so well; the untapped confidence and ability to lean into whatever they desire.

After watching her for the last hour, I spot the differences so easily. Mel is a calming, rainy day that turns into a storm we all sensed coming, that strikes fast and hard, while Raven is a constant grumbling thunder. Mel keeps her fangs out in the open while Raven hides hers behind a pretty smile and too much lipstick.

The problem is, I don't like sharing my doll with anyone else, and I don't really want to play with this one.

Ensuring my mask is tight over my head, I swirl the glass of bubbling wine and walk toward her. "You look like you could use a few of those."

Raven's ocean eyes glitter at the glass, then the paddle in her hand. "I could use a bit of both." She takes the offered wine, tosses it back, then hands me the rounded paddle.

The one thing about Mel's *medicine* is that it must be ingested in small doses, and Raven just drank the entire bag.

Chapter Nine

"You can't tell me to figure out why Hayse has overseas connections when he is a prince in a kingdom that has overseas connections!" I shove my finger deep into Dragon's chest. "And let's not forget that little piece of information you conveniently failed to mention. The false prince? Do you know the danger you put me in by letting me walk in blind?"

It's been a week and I'm still fuming. From waking up in my bed with throbbing nipples without any idea how I got there, and Raven vomiting with a fever that has her both sweating and shivering uncontrollably, my nerves are a wreck.

"You've dealt with false royals before. What's the problem this time?"

"All eyes are on him!" I pinch the ridge of my nose. Complaining isn't going to help me when I've already come to terms with my situation. "There is no problem now that I know, but I need more. A name or anything to go on to help me lead a conversation."

Dragon dips his chin as if I let him down. "I'm merely curious why royals would want to deal with a false prince and not Percival directly."

"What deals?" I ask.

Dragon's head tilts in a way that has my stomach twisting with unease. He won't hurt me because of Duke, but part of me isn't entirely convinced. This man is physically terrifying to be in the presence of with the black, hooded cloak and dragon mask that hides every inch of him, not to mention his reputation for torture. "How close are you to your father?" His tone isn't solely curious, it's pressing.

I look around the forest, the slits in my devilish mask making it harder to fully take in my surroundings. When I'm sure there's no one lurking around, I whisper, "What does my father have to do with any of this?"

"Maybe nothing," he shrugs, "but with the Aramos and Deimos in alliance with the overseas kings, I figured you would know more than I do."

"My father doesn't..." I bite my tongue to keep myself from explaining that my father doesn't use me for Deimos information, not after using what he needed to secure the gold-tight alliance. "He doesn't tell me about his deals."

"Forget it. Your potential knowledge is half the reason I asked for you anyway. Your reputation is quiet but known." His gloved fingers graze the cheek of my mask lovingly. "You're my temptress, so tempt him."

My eyes hit the sky. "How do I tempt someone who has no interest in me? All he wants to do is punish me. Fuck *with* me, not fuck me."

Dragon's shoulders shake with quiet laughter.

"What's so funny?"

"Oh, doll, he wants you. Don't get me wrong, I'm sure there are some men who don't, but those men prefer something heavier between their lover's legs." He pauses. "I didn't take you for someone to be easily thrown by a little challenge."

"I'm not easily thrown from it!" I turn, needing a second to pull my thoughts together. "He just—"

"Isn't like other men?" I can hear the sarcasm in his voice. The reminder of his warning during our first meeting.

"I'll get you more information." I let out a heavy sigh. "I just... It's not going to be from Hayse."

Dragon's spine snaps straight. "Why not Hayse?"

"It's supposed to be kept quiet, but my father is coming to meet with the other alliances, which means I'll have access to the overseas kings you want me to look into."

"No!" Dragon steps forward, reaching to grab me, but I'm too quick and step back before he gets a chance. "Your task is Hayse, Percival too, for that matter, but no one else. Do you understand? I don't want you that deep."

"It's fine." I wave him off. "I've met with most of them before. My father is meticulous about who he deals with."

Audrey, my sister-in-law, wraps her arms around my neck with a loud squeal. It's the best greeting I could have gotten from anyone in my family besides Eva, who, thank all the stars, woke up the day after I left. She stayed back to heal and hide out from my father, who attempted to murder her husband. Something no one has the full story on yet.

I can feel Audrey's bump as she pulls back from our tight embrace. I couldn't be happier for her and my brother. Their journey together isn't a happy one, but they made it and they deserve as many children as they wish.

Audrey is the one person I want to take aside and talk to right now, but that conversation will have to wait. With a stiff scowl, my father beckons me to where he's sitting at breakfast, taking in every person who walks through the door with paranoid assessment. He's dangerously close to one of his episodes, and I pray that it starts after he leaves.

The sound of my heels brings his attention back to me until I'm close enough for him to yank me down next to him. "Jax will be arriving today. Do what you must to find out why the pirates have an interest in the false prince."

"Hayse?" I jerk away, quickly pulled back into him. My wrist wails from how tightly he's holding me.

"Do we ask questions?"

I shake my head with a quick answer. "No, no. I didn't. I'll do it."

"Yes, you will. Tonight." He lets me go, muttering something into his glass. I take that as a sign to walk away as fast as I can before he pulls me into anything else.

I return to Audrey, narrowing my suspicion on the sparkling orange juice my brother hands me. "You haven't died yet."

"Your disappointment wounds me," I tell him, grimacing at the sour flavor in the flute. I look around in search of Oliver so I can bribe him into pouring me the vintage malbec from the cellar. I refuse to sit through another feast with despicable people and even shittier wine. Breakfast or not, with my serenade snuff disappearing, I'll need as much of this as I can get.

"And me." Audrey shoves Cain's shoulder to behave.

"Finally tiring of him?" I give her a wink and lift the strap of her dress, reminding her of the time she made this exact same move on me. "Speaking of despisable men, how do you seduce a man who isn't interested in you?"

Cain chokes on his drink, his palm wiping what spilled down his chin.

"Mel, you can't be serious?" Audrey laughs, the soft greens in her eyes glimmering with amusement. "You had my nipple in your mouth when I was in love with your brother. Trust me, whoever this is, has already lost a game he doesn't know he's playing."

"Or has a brain." Audrey elbows Cain again. "I'm not reliving one of the worst moments of my life." He walks away in the direction I saw Oliver headed when I start telling Audrey about all my attempts at seducing Hayse and his constant dismissals, keeping it vague enough to keep his identity hidden.

"It sounds like you enjoy it, or you would have used your safe word." Her grin spreads.

"This isn't about me." I quickly turn it around before we can dissect why I haven't used my word. He's had me in two situations where I should have shouted it, but not knowing what he's going to do next fills me with a feeling I can't explain, something that buries the word deep in my mind.

"Of course it is. He's edging you." She giggles into her palm. "And your bratty behavior is only going to keep riling him up."

"So don't be a brat?" *Impossible.*

My best strategy is to stay far away from Hayse. He's too much of a distraction. When I'm with him, I'm not focused on getting any information but on winning his annoying game of *edging*, as Audrey called it.

The fact that my father and Dragon want the same information isn't lost on me, but I ignore the nagging in the back of my head because it's working in my favor now that I have someone else to seek information from.

As we take our seats, I notice neither Hayse nor Percival are present, which sends alarms off in my head. A royal greeting without either prince isn't just odd, it's rude, damn near disrespectful.

Without wives at their sides, King Hale Deimos and Sterling Soren look more like lovers as they greet both real and false royals who arrived this morning, all of whom I'm assessing to figure out which ones I want to target after Jax.

It could be because I'm faced with another coincidence, or the fact that I'm a royal flirting with death by going after Hayse, but when I look at the kings again, a question arises that I've never considered before. What are the chances their wives perished and neither of them remarried?

As plates are passed around, I'm left unserved again. This time, I don't let any rumors start flying before I loudly announce that I'm not impressed by the lack of flavor in this kingdom's bland food and excuse myself.

My father's anger is visible in his red cheeks as I drag my chair back farther than necessary, making a point to refill my glass, and smacking my heels out of the great hall.

The sound of small feet echo behind me and it's not just the scaly girl peeking around the walls this time, but two more. A boy with features I can only describe as lizard-like, with his sharp, pointy chin and round eyes. The second girl has a prominent uptick in her nose, a cute little piggish button.

It hits me who these kids are once I see their plain clothes and fingers wrinkled from soaking water. *The mice in the walls*, they're called. Most kingdoms have ears, usually servants or rumors of ghosts, but the Deimos have orphan children that the servants raise to eventually replace them.

They squeal when I wave.

"She *is* pretty," the piggish one whispers.

"It's children's blood that keeps her hair like that," the boy says. "She eats them."

"Only the naughty ones," I shout over my shoulder and turn a corner, unable to contain my giggles.

I might have had too much wine without any food in my belly.

"Eat, Mi Vera." Percival hands me and Raven full plates of food, where we're snuggled in bed. The entire day was spent drinking between napping and her trying to get me to think through my plans better. I detest plans. I'm more of a *do-and-hope-for-the-best* kind of girl.

Raven covers her nose and mouth, rushing toward the washroom.

Percival's brown eyes soften as he shoves one plate on my lap and the other on the nightstand. "I promise the seasonings will be to your liking." His grin tightens, and I let out a small laugh. He's known me too long and too intimately to have bought a single word I said, but he also knows me well enough to trust that I would have said such a thing.

As I take a closer look at him, he looks a little pale, too. "Long day of training." He waves off my concern and continues, "I'd stay, but I have to sit in on the royal meetings. You should probably stay in here tonight. Blair's aunts are still furious with you for starting that fire, and with the overseas kingdoms around…" He pauses, his handsome face shifting into concern. "There's a lot of tension that our fathers are trying to smooth over."

"And you don't need me making it worse?"

His ear kisses his shoulder. "Honestly, yeah. They're more dangerous than you think."

I do my best to reassure him that I'll be fine without actually promising to stay. He doesn't look convinced but warns me again to eat, promising a bottle of their oldest wine if I behave.

Little does he know, I snagged that before taking my first nap.

"Could you come by later instead?" I lean into his arm and give him a needy look that he reciprocates.

"Do you ever need to ask?" He pulls my chin so we're close enough that I can smell the mint on his breath. I won't be able to wait one more day before I resort to asking Raven to help me with the edge Hayse left me on. My fingers aren't going to be enough this time.

I shake my head and bridge the gap, planting my lips on his. His hand falls to my hair as he opens, deepening the kiss with a passion only he possesses.

"I'll meet you at the Den." He leaves with the promise that does no favors in relieving the ache constantly buzzing through me.

I wait until Raven has eaten before I go, leaving her my untouched plate after tucking her into bed and ensuring she has water by the nightstand. I hate leaving her behind when she's sick, but I have to make the most of my time while the royals are here, and I already lost an entire day because I drank too much.

The visiting quarters are a floor below. The first few stairs are easy, but my vision blurs as I take the first turn down the spiraling staircase. I may not mind the dark, but I do have an intense fear of heights, and with the lack of food in my belly, the distance I see below me is messing with my head. Gripping the rail, I take in a deep breath and finish the rest of the steps as fast as I can.

The moment I step onto the visiting level, the energy makes my skin crawl. Knowing what I'm about to do and what I may have to do with others if this lead doesn't work out, I lift my chin and ready myself to make this visit as brief as possible.

Jax's room is the farthest door on the right, taking me past aggressive arguments, heated moans, and thick snores behind closed and cracked doors.

My stomach tightens with every step, my palms growing sweaty. I don't have what I need here to make the serenade snuff, so I have to go into this with my real mind, not the one I temper with powder. I'm in a relaxed haze after one sniff, but two allows me to hold my tongue and not fight my natural instinct to argue or fight back. When I'm seducing, one does the trick. If the man's grotesquery runs deeper than appearances, he gets more than a little sprinkled in his cup.

Raven...

I should have noticed the signs. The poor girl is going to be out of it for a while, but karma isn't known for her kindness. She should have asked. Then again, I did tell her, '*What's mine is yours.*'

I'll deal with her later.

My hand is over the handle of Jax's door when I hear a familiar voice order, "Make it quick."

My head snaps to the door behind me. "I have always wanted to be with a prince. A royal—"

"Just hurry the fuck up," Hayse barks.

I shouldn't… But I'm going to.

My palm is too sweaty and barely able to grip the knob to turn it, but by some miracle I do manage to without making so much as a creak. The small crack gives me all I need to see a sight that has my cheeks burning.

Hayse chugs from a bottle of wine, dropping it lazily at his side as his head leans against the back of the winged back chair. A man kneels between his legs, his head bobbing up and down, giving him his best.

Hayse isn't looking. He doesn't even look as if he notices someone sucking him down. If I weren't staring at the man working hard, I would have thought Hayse had dozed off in the chair.

"Does his Majesty—"

"Stop talking," Hayse grumbles with a hate-filled sneer.

I draw in a venomous breath at hearing the hate I thought was reserved only for me.

I nearly gasp again when Hayse's eyes lift, latching onto mine.

Fuck.

I'm stuck.

I can't turn away and pretend I didn't see this, not when he's glaring at me with shifty eyes. He blinks a few times as if he's trying to rid me of his vision, but after the last one, his entire face shifts into something dark and alluring.

The bottle clanks to the floor, wine pooling under the man's knees as Hayse grips his hair.

My mouth waters at the sight. It shouldn't, but it makes sense why he doesn't want me. He prefers the company of men. A prickle of irritation doesn't just poke at me but suffocates my entire being.

Shame. I feel ashamed that I let myself believe Audrey was right, that this was some long game when, in reality, I had it right all along. He really was just fucking with me—humiliating me. He was never planning on being with me in that way.

Hayse's hips buck. The man struggles, but Hayse holds him in place. "Stay there, wicked one." Those soulless eyes are stuck on me, watching me as he drives into the man's mouth.

I can't stop, can't look away, can't so much as breathe. His chest rises and falls, his lips parting as he finishes.

When he releases his hold on the man's head, I turn and rush into Jax's room, slamming the door behind me, holding it with my back.

What the hell was that?

The pirate looks at me with a raised brow. "I shouldn't even be surprised that you're here. What is it you need to know, princess?" His dimples deepen at my sudden surprise. "You lost for words? I never would have thought I'd see the day."

Jax stands from the bed, his pirate appearance grungier than ever with his long black hair tied at the nape of his neck, tattoos scattered around his narrow frame, his shirt always halfway buttoned down revealing his sunbathed skin. All of it was something that once made me drool and bend anyway he told me to. He is a seduction I've always enjoyed, but as he lifts his shirt over his head, I can't find myself ogling him.

Snapping out of whatever trance Hayse had me in, I meet Jax's sheepish grin, giving him one of my own. "There she is. Let's hear it, love." The scruff on his chin grazes my temple as he leans into my neck, his hand gripping my waist as the other pulls at my corset strings.

"Who is that across the hall from you?" My voice is heavy as he tosses my corset to the side. He's always been fast with his fingers.

"Walk on something you didn't want to?" His snort makes my head spin. "Another pirate who spent a lot of money on the scene you just saw."

We both hiss as his fingers graze my breast. He pulls back to lift my chemise over my head, his eyes lighting at the sight of the spikes through my nipples. "She never had these."

I catch the loss in his eyes and grab his cheeks before he can think too much about *her*—his little sprite—someone he lost and has been searching for years to find. A girl who looks and acts, coincidentally, exactly like me—tiny, blonde, and fiery, as he puts it.

"Focus, Jax." I hold his head between my hands. "*Elijah*, I need you to tell me everything you know about Hayse Soren. Why does that pirate want him?"

He shrugs, stepping back and lazily drops onto the bed. His mood sours when he starts thinking about her. "It's the auction. What else is there to know?"

"What auction?" I gather my clothes and redress, leaning against the desk to give him the space he needs from me.

"The auction." There's uncertainty behind his voice, like he's confused at my confusion. "How don't you know about the auction? You and Hayse have been at the top of the list for years. Until now, I suppose." His rugged features twist, deepening his concern as he jumps back to his feet, growing more alert and distressed. "You're telling me you haven't known that you've been bought and sold repeatedly over the years?"

I shake my head, the fast motion giving me a head rush.

"It's exclusive." His tone switches to apologetic so easily though he still carries unease in his stiff shoulders. "It's a royal fucking mess, to be honest. It's the latest I've been looking into to find *her*. Someone said she was among those listed before she disappeared. That pirate across the hall recently filled me in. Nearly cost me a hand and a foot, practically sold my soul to be in the know."

My mind rushes through too many questions: What exactly is this auction, and how did I get on this list? Is this... I shake the last one away. There has to be a mistake.

"This was both of your last rounds with the upcoming wedding, and whoever bought you spent *a lot* of money. Fuck!" He pulls his hair from the tie and runs his hands through it. "This changes everything. I thought... We're told that everyone on that list agreed and is selling themselves for the money."

If Hayse is getting serviced now, then whoever bought me is here, too. I should be more angry, but the vain part of me wonders how much I'm worth.

"Thank you." I reach for him, grabbing his arm. "If you want, I can still—"

He shakes his head.

"I'm sorry, Jax. I hope you find her." The dagger at his hip catches my attention with a horrible idea I can't push away. "Do you still know how to stitch?"

He looks me over, then grins, dropping his slacks to show a set of fresh jagged seams, sewn lazily along his thighs. "Not very well."

"Perfect."

Chapter Ten

"Mel!" Blair calls my name from down the hall, rushing toward me with too much enthusiasm. "Where are you going?" Her mouth drops at the bandages on my forehead. Being the polite girl she is, she quickly schools her features as if nothing is there.

"Looking for Hayse and Percival. Have you seen them?" She follows at my side as we near their rooms. Something about her is off. It takes me a second to grasp that it's her outfit. She's in a simple yet elegant obsidian dress with a matching corset, and headband embedded atop her golden locks. It's an outfit I would wear. I give her an impressed nod. She's starting to look more and more like me every day.

Her cheeks turn a bright shade of pink. "They left."

"Oh?" I give her a look that tells her to go on.

"I'll only tell you if you take me with you."

Well damn, she's starting to act like me too. "You got me. Spill."

She looks up and down the hall before leaning into me with the softest whisper. "They went to the Forbidden Den."

I already knew, but seeing her squirm was worth playing dumb. She also isn't as strait-laced as I thought if she's willingly intrigued to come.

I almost feel bad asking, "Do you own anything lacy?"

I much prefer Raven at my side compared to the bouncy girl next to me who can't choose which scene she's more fascinated by, the spanking, the fucking, or… okay, even I'm confused by the one bleeding in the corner until I remember Raven saying something about the euphoria that comes with the loss of blood, the weightlessness and loss of control, tempting death.

I should tell them that all they need to do is not eat for a few days to achieve that.

The thick scents lift me lighter as I take Blair to the bar and tell her to stay put. The blush, lace slip makes her appear more childish in my opinion, even though she's the same age as I am. She's cute and innocent in all the wrong ways.

I don't have to look around to find Hayse in the same spot I saw him the first time, relaxed on the round chaise, watching others around him with a spliff hanging from his lips. As I approach, he looks me up and down, taking in the black glittering quarter-mask that covers my forehead and matches the sliver of fabric that barely covers the most intimate parts of me, before turning his attention back to the others. "Not now."

"I need to talk—"

"I said not now!" His voice is cold and harsh, cutting me a glare that makes me want to crawl into a hole and hide.

"*Fuck. You.*" I look around but don't see Percival anywhere.

It's fine. I came here to scratch an itch before I harass Hayse with questions anyway, hoping all the pent-up energy he's built will knock some sense back in me once it's released.

Turning with a toss of my hair, I grab the first woman I see and nudge her onto an empty chaise, not bothering with the seduction before I glue my lips to hers. Her tongue slides into mine with ease, her hands sliding around my hips and up my spine.

I can feel Hayse's eyes on my back more than I feel the woman's skin on mine. The issue is, I'm not enjoying this. I used to be able to trick myself into feeling powerful and needed when I'm on top, using others' bodies to bring them pleasure, thinking it's only me who can do it for them, but as the woman groans against my lips, I find no joy in it.

It's so basic and boring when I know what's coming next.

The hair on my scalp tightens. "Do you have a glutton for punishment?" At Hayse's voice, the girl rolls out from under me and runs off. I'm pulled back to my knees only to be picked up by my hips and tossed over his shoulder. His hand comes down hard on my ass. "No show this time."

A girl we pass sighs and pouts as he carries me toward the back. I seal my eyes the entire way to keep my stomach from turning over at the height he holds me.

Once I hear a door shut, I barely get my eyes open before I'm flung onto a bed. Hayse's chest rises and falls at an unsteady rhythm with that hateful scowl I want so badly to sit on.

He's pissed. I bite my smile at the sight of his sadistic serpent uncoiling from within to greet me again.

"Seems a bit over-reactive when you had your cock down another throat an hour ago."

"Turn around and bend over."

"No." I cross my arms over my chest, wincing as I rub against the sharp, tickling pain under my brassiere. All it does is remind me that I hate this man even more than I did two seconds ago. "Not until you tell me why you were with that man."

My priorities need to be rearranged.

He leans down and forces my arms to my side. A white lock falls over his dead eyes.

"If you prefer men, why are you messing with me?" Okay, now I want to hide because is that actual jealousy in my voice?

His lip curls, catching the same shameful tone I did. "A hole's a hole."

"You just don't want mine."

That tilted smirk widens with the tightening of his grip around my wrists. "Your holes were mine the second you let me take that cane to you."

"Then why?!" I raise myself as high as I can from the sitting position, shifting to my knees so we're an inch apart. "Why be with that man? Why—"

"I don't have a choice." His words are rushed and for some reason they piss me off.

"*You* don't have a choice?" I scoff. It's the lack of food. The lack of medicinal snuff. The laugh that leaves me isn't my own. "You? Do you know what it's like to be used like a fucking doll just so your father knows something others don't? To seduce a woman you learn is your brother's lover because your father has a sick fucked-up mind?"

He sent me after Audrey at my brother's ball so Cain would walk in and see the '*whore*' she really is, only I didn't know who she was. I was told to do what it took to get her into bed, or I'd be chained away again.

"Royals, kings, princes, knights, guards, fucking bakers…" I shove him back so hard he stumbles. "All for what? For an edge-up? To barter deals? All the while, there's been an auction that's sold away my body without me knowing. Did you know?" I grab the collar of his shirt. "I never had a real choice, but I never thought… Did you know our fathers sold us?"

I've had an hour to think through this. He had to have known. He didn't appear to want to be with that man, and the only person who could make me do anything like that has always been my father. Hayse is like me in too many ways. His demons compliment mine too well.

I always thought I had a choice in being with those my father sent me to, and I gaslit myself into believing it. Knowing about this auction is making me second-guess everything. Did every man buy me, and my father took advantage by having me seduce secrets? Were the secrets a ploy to get me to cooperate after I rejected the first man so fiercely?

I did everything I could to repress my early memories, mixing and creating anything I could until I found my serenade snuff.

Hayse's jaw tightens. I'm not looking down and I'm not sure when he let me go but I thank whatever guardian demon is watching over me when I hear his knuckles pop from how hard he's clenching his fists. "Bend the *fuck* over, Mel."

Something snaps in me, some cord that contains what little care I have left in this world. I turn around and do exactly as he says, resting my head on the pillow because I'm too tired to hold myself up.

The first smack rocks me forward. My toes curl at the sting. "Tell me you're sorry."

"*Umph…* I'm sorry." I don't know what for, but I am. As his hand comes down harder, I cry out, repeating how sorry I am, again and again, as his punishing palm finds a new patch of flesh to bruise.

I'm ready for another smack when his fingers press against my soaked center. "Your body is weeping for me, wicked one." He grunts, giving me another slap lower this time. "I don't think you mind being *my* doll."

Why does it feel like he's trying to find my limits? Do I have those? As the pain increases, I don't care to remember my safe word. That feeling I was hoping to find by climbing on top of that woman is ten times over.

His fingers trail through my hair, gripping at the crown of my skull, bringing my head against his chest. "Open."

His head falls back with the bottle of wine lifting to his lips. He doesn't take much before he drops the bottle and wraps his fingers around my throat. Wine drips down his chin just before he purses his lips and spits it into my mouth. He watches me swallow the sweet red, hovering a breath away from my lips that ache for his. "You don't even know how perfect you are like this."

A heavy moan leaves my throat. I don't know what's wrong with me that I find more joy in him punishing and praising me than sex with any others I've ever been with. Every slap he gives me feels deserved in the most heinous way.

I flop back to the bed, waiting for the next one, tensing, knowing it's any second before he hits me again, when something wet and cold is rubbed over me instead. The cool lotion soothes my burning skin, relaxing me flat onto the covers. "You're going to be good for me a little longer." He brushes the hair from my face as he sits beside me and pulls me into his lap for a better angle to keep soothing the sting.

His fingers dip between my legs, feeling what his depravity does to me. Humiliation rushes to my cheeks. I turn my head, but Hayse stops me. "Don't hide from me, pretty girl."

"Wha—" My back arches as his finger slides to my back entrance.

"You sounded jealous when you talked about me not using your holes." He twirls his finger in circles, teasing me. "Relax."

I try, but every time he gets a little farther in, I clench back up, the feeling foreign and uncomfortable. "You take everything I give you so fucking perfect."

That heavy moan leaves my chest at his approval. It's addicting. My mind turns to mush, and the world around me spins into a hazy mess.

His fingers find their rhythm, no longer painful or uncomfortable, but a new sense of pleasure that I'm working to understand.

"Open." Metal rubs along my tongue and is gone before I get a chance to see what it was. "You're going to wear this until I take it out for you." His fingers are gone, replaced by that cold metal pressing into me.

"Hayse…"

"You can always say your safe word."

And lose? No, thank you.

As he works the metal into me, my breath grows heavy while the room tilts again. My stomach growls so hard I feel it shake against his lap.

"Did you not eat?" Hayse's palm is on my cheek, but I barely feel it. "What the fuck? Percival was supposed to—" He huffs in frustration. "Don't move."

The door opens and I reach for the wine he dropped on the floor, wrapping my lips around the opening when the door shuts. Seeing Hayse coming back for me, I drop it, offering it to him first.

He shakes his head. "I don't drink."

"Oh." I let it tumble back to the floor as he drops beside me, bringing my head to his lap and turns me to face him. "But I saw—"

"*Open*," he cuts me off. I know that look and keep my prying to myself. His drink is my snuff, reserved for special situations.

"Why do you care?" I groan through the exhaustion. All my focus remains on the foreign object inside of me. Again, it doesn't hurt, but it's strange to have something just… there.

"I don't." He orders me to open again, this time twisting my nipple, which does the trick. As he drops a blackberry into my mouth, he continues. "In fact, it's quite the opposite. I'm just ensuring you don't pass out on me. Some people are into that, but I'm not. I want you to be aware of every second I play with you."

The third blackberry bursts into my mouth, and for as long as he's feeding them to me, I understand why people believe in things such as Gods and Heavens while cursing us damned souls with our black-hearts and hellish attitudes.

"We should stop. Whatever this is. This game…" He pops another blackberry into my mouth to shut me up, but I can't push aside the guilt. Sex is one thing, but whatever this is… it's different. For me, anyway. "You're with Blair."

"And you're already married to Percival. What's the problem?"

"Blair," I answer honestly. "She's sweet and innocent. She's good."

"So are you." His smirk has me reaching for a blackberry on my own. "Do you think I want someone like her?" He holds the fruit away from my reach.

"Yeah. With your tendencies, don't you want to break her? I'm already—"

"I don't want to break a good girl, beautiful." He lifts my chin. "I want to make a good girl out of a bad one."

Hayse

Sweat pours down my forehead as I take my final lap around the palace, followed by as many pushups, sit-ups, and pull-ups it takes until I'm throwing up behind a tree. It doesn't leave me as sore as I need, but it's enough to exude all the pent-up energy I'm causing myself.

Most people might turn to vices like wine, drugs, or women, but this is my preferred way of dealing with things—*most* things. I never wanted to end up like Hale or Sterling, or any king who drinks too much wine while counting their riches. I've always sought purpose, a reason to wake up every day.

Perfecting my body has always given me something to focus on. Drawing was another, tinkering with things. So long as I keep my hands busy, I have a reason for the next day.

Now, it's Mel. The cause of my pent-up energy, but also my newest reason to wake up. She is the only person who can make riches look effortless. The only person I don't mind seeing with a drink or adorned in jewels, not just because she's irresistible and looks unholy and flawless with them, but because she won't be able to enjoy any of those things she loves much longer.

Making my way through the back entrance, I ignore the passing waves and flirty smiles. I don't bother knocking before I throw open Percival's door and kick it shut behind me. "We have a problem."

"You're telling me." Percival hands me the healing salve and tosses his shirt across the room. "It was the last one, so they made sure to make it hurt."

Black bruises mark his entire torso, lacerations cut into the meat of his thighs, and his eyes are dark and heavy.

"*Fuck*. I'm sorry, man. I—"

"Don't worry about it," he cuts me off. "You still went through with it. It doesn't matter how harsh you were to him or how quick you popped off." He snickers as I paste him up, trying to rid myself of another disgusting memory of being used. "At least you know what's coming."

We've been through this too many times for me to care. I always know what's coming. Percival thinks I have it as easy as he does, and I let him believe it, but the truth is, I get double the punishment because I'm the false prince, the face of the Deimos Kingdom.

My name might technically be Hayse Soren, but to everyone outside of the inner circle, I'm Percival Deimos, the royal prince and heir to the Deimos family. The one they buy while using the real one, my friend, as bait to keep me in line.

"She knows about the auction."

Percival halts my rubbing, his pretty face souring. If we're going by looks, Percival should be the face. He has girls dropping to their knees the second he walks into the Forbidden Den, while they want me because I don't give it to them. I take who I want at random, not recently because of a particular silvery-blonde toy that arrived, but I'm the unachievable challenge. And when they do get a taste of me? They fucking run. I haven't found anyone who can take what I give to the full extent I need.

"How did she find out?"

"I don't know, and I don't care. That's not the problem." I push him to the bed and continue rubbing the salve over him, noting every wince and groan as I tell him exactly what she told me, word for word.

He's only this fucked up because I didn't spend the entire night with the man. When I was finished, I left to follow the wicked one, but she was already gone.

"She was on the list? But—"

"She's been on the list." I correct him, showing him just how surprised I was when she told me. When Mel started spiraling, I had to mask my utter shock by not only that, but how she sounded as if she hated seducing people for their secrets.

I know who she is and what she does.

I hate her for it.

I've never hated anyone as much as I hate Amelvira Lunasol Aramos. I'm not superstitious, but I've muttered curses and hexes her way here and there throughout the years. Once, I even saw a straw doll with blonde hair and stuck a pin in it.

All I want is to bring her to her knees in the worst way. Humiliate her, own her, make her into the toy she's made me over the years because of the secrets she's spilled.

She's mine. My personal fucking toy I'm going to ruin and break over and over again until she's begging me to end her life once and for all. And when she does, I'll do it all over again.

I would have enjoyed ending her life before I learned how much I love playing with her. Her body was made for me. Her mind, too, how she doesn't use her safe word, even though I've seen it flutter behind her eyes when it's too much. It's why I keep using the restraints. Those are the only weaknesses I've been able to find in her.

And then there's that wicked tongue I push her to use just to tame and punish her more. She's such a perfect girl every time, taking every single thing I give her, somehow brattier and more defiant the next time, playing through the routine I need all over again.

I'm addicted to how she lets me push her further and further. Making her crawl for me was just the start.

I wasn't planning to pierce her until I had her in my bed and felt an overbearing need to mark her in some way. Just when I thought she was going to break, she moaned. I don't even think she knew she did it, and still does it when the pain hits her at a certain level. I know the level it takes to hear it. It's my favorite song.

Maybe that's why I took her to the back room tonight. I don't want others to hear it. It's mine.

She's mine.

I didn't want her trust, but I love that I have it. It's the praises, the way she submits further with every one I give her. I *want* to give them to her after she makes those ridiculous public scenes. She doesn't take shit from anyone. I'm livid I missed the chair screeching at breakfast.

My anger flares at the thought.

Whoever is pulling strings to keep her from being fed is my real enemy because I meant it when I said I don't want her passing out on me. If I have to feed her blackberries—yes, I learned her favorite food, and yes, I ensured the Forbidden Den had it stocked so she's as comfortable there as possible—I'll pick them myself, suffer all the thorns to ensure she's eaten. A rat falls for the trap with cheese after all.

I toss the empty salve tin back at Percival.

"Our problem is, who the fuck bought her?"

Chapter Eleven

I thought I hated Hayse before, but walking around with something metal inside a part of me that tightens too much throughout the day is making me think up stronger words for my growing loathing—that's not a strong enough term either.

It's not that it hurts, it's not knowing what's coming. I have this constant pull in my lower belly that heats every time I attempt to sit or put too much pressure into my steps, remembering his fingers and hands doing filthy things to me while his praises in that deep husky voice melted me into a puddle of fine wine.

Raven bit her lip to keep from laughing when I told her. "Have a few drinks and you'll forget it's there."

While doing our best to avoid my father by taking up a corner behind a loud group of girls, *a few* turned into five glasses of the infamous Deimos pinot noir, and it's beginning to feel like this drab feast is in need of a little excitement. I'd hate for my admirers to be disappointed.

"Please don't." Cain steps beside me with Audrey on his arm. They remind me so much of Eva and her husband, both beautiful women, able to take care of themselves with men who would burn the world around them to ensure they never have to again.

It's envious. To have someone love you so deeply that they would kill for you. To love someone so much you'd slit your own throat to save them.

"Come on," I groan, motioning toward the violinist I wish were a pianist, the flowery blush décor that nearly burns my eyes with its soft, childish hue, and the porcelain statue molded into an elegant Blair looking to the sky with a gleaming, angelic smile. "They act like it's a holy holiday."

The fifteen-layered cake sits on full display in the center with far too many candles. It takes someone who thinks about doing something irresponsible to see the slight lean it has, the possibility of a disaster under just the right circumstances.

Blair stands beside it, matching the periwinkle frosting perfectly, her smile brighter than the flames that will light the massive desert. When her eyes land on mine, I plant a matching smile and return her eager wave. If I didn't, I'm sure she'd cry.

I can hear her aunt Florence's rambling from here. "It was nothing. It practically made itself——"

"Can you ever be happy for someone else, or does it always have to be about you?"

My head snaps toward my brother's sharp tone. Facing him straight on, I ask the one thing we've always danced around. "Why do you hate me?"

Audrey audibly sucks in a shallow breath and threads her arm through Raven's, suggesting they get another round of drinks.

"Wow." Cain rocks on his heels, sneering into his glass. "After all these years, you finally care enough to ask. As if you don't already know."

"For the sake of argument, Cain, just tell me. You were never around when we were children, so what could I have possibly done?"

"You're just like *him*." He nods behind me. I don't have to look to know who he's talking about. Cain never loses his temper unless he's discussing our father. "You have the same disregard for others and act like you own every room you walk into. You breathe chaos and disruption, wreaking havoc on everyone's lives. Just like you did sixteen years ago. You'll never change."

"Well, go on." I wave my empty glass between us. "Let me hear what horrible thing I did sixteen years ago when I was..." I look to the gaudy crown molding in thought. "Seven? Eight?"

"You told Father about Audrey!" He clears his throat and looks around to ensure he isn't loud enough to cause a scene. I, on the other hand, couldn't care less. The tension between us has always been palpable. "You told him she was in my room that night, and it's what put her in that hell of a life all these years, what made my daughters grow up without their father!" His cheeks redden. "I didn't get to see them grow up because of you!"

"I've never seen any woman in your room." I keep my voice as low and tight as I can while a hurt that I didn't realize I still carried slices through my heart. My own brother thinks I'm cruel enough to rat him out, *knowing* what our father is capable of.

Lifting my chin, I do what I do best. "If I'm honest. I would have thought you went the other way with all that extra training."

"Don't try to get out of this by jesting." His lips curl with cruel determination. "I heard you telling Eva about finding a girl—"

I slam my hand over his mouth. My eyes widen, looking around the hall until I find my father in deep conversation with the other kings. I can't even take in my surprise to see King Whitehart next to him, chatting as if my father hadn't blown his manner to pieces weeks ago. "Cain, you can never speak of that. That wasn't... It wasn't about you."

His brows pinch, peeling my hand away. "I don't believe you."

"Ask Eva."

"I'm asking *you*." Knowing the reason he's despised me all these years, I *let* him keep the firm grip around my wrist. If only because he's never asked me anything.

I let out a deep sigh. "It was the night I learned about Father's episodes."

His head jerks back with confusion. "What episodes?"

"You know... When Mrs. Platewell sends Father away for a few weeks, sometimes months, or when he... Cain, I can't. Not here."

"Amelvira, if you don't tell me what the hell has been going on right now, I swear on the Devil that spawned you, I'll throw you right back to the place everyone wishes you returned to."

He's always known how to get me to smile. My teeth bite into the pillow of my lip to keep from laughing out loud. Taking his untouched wine, I toss it back, grimacing at the dryness along my tongue, and begin before I can change my mind.

"Sixteen years ago, I found a woman in the basement. I told Mrs. Platewell, but she told me I was going stir-crazy from all of Father's trainings," I continue without a breath and a voice that doesn't match the horrors I'm about to tell him, "The following week, Father brought me here with him when he made his alliance with Deimos. He said since I was so good at sneaking around and uncovering secrets, I could put it to good use. That led to my marriage to Percival, and he hasn't stopped since. When his episodes get too bad before Mrs. Platewell can send him away, he turns to me. He sees and hears things that aren't there. He thinks I'm mom..." My voice catches in my throat, but I shake it off before those memories can resurface, gripping the scar along my stomach. "It wasn't until Eva disappeared that I found Silas in the basement."

I peek back at Whitehart, Soren, Deimos, and my father, wondering how these kings can brutalize one another, each other's families and land, and still crack a smile while sipping wine.

"He was on the edge of death," I quickly add. "He was whipped so brutally, Cain. Father forgot about him because that episode escalated too quickly before Mrs. Platewell could step in."

His face gives nothing away but his hold on my elbow is everything. My brother doesn't touch anyone unless it's to shed blood. The unfamiliar softness in his touch causes me to grimace. His jaw shifts, moving like he doesn't know where to start first. "Are you telling me you're already married to Percival?"

"Since I was eight."

"That fucking—" He motions to a far corner behind him. "And what about him?" Percival and Hayse are surrounded by Blair and her three aunts, sending my heart fluttering with laughter. Knowing Hayse's true nature, his charming mask looks miserable until he spots me. The metal inside me is the only thing I can feel as his eyes flare with something that isn't *just* hate. "Does he have you doing anything you don't want to?"

I yank my arm from his hold and straighten my deep blue dress. I hate it, but it's Percival's color, just like Blair is in pink, a shade of Hayse's preferred red. "Knowing the dirty details of my life is a bit vulgar for you—" I start before refocusing on the scene behind him.

It's Margarette. Her teal dress is brighter than usual, complimented by the golden rings on her fingers and the chain around her neck. Her graying, black hair is tucked back into her matching headband as she hauls a little girl away by her arm.

I don't need to hear a single word. The sharp *slap* has my heels nearly breaking with the force I'm stomping toward them. Heads turn, but all I see is the black tunnelling my vision.

"Margarette?" I use my delicate voice. As she turns, there's a distasteful surprise that hits her face before I do. Her cheeks are puffy, but that doesn't stop the loud grunt or the stinging *crack* that kills every conversation, laughter, or whisper.

I take the scaley girl's hand into my throbbing one, tightly, before she can run away.

"Sorry, I thought I saw a fly on your cheek. I can see why it confused you for a musty pile of shit." Leaning into her ear so only she can hear, I vow with every fiber of my being, "Enjoy the night. It'll be your last."

Looking down at the scaly girl, I smile. "I have something to show you."

She keeps up as I pull her out of the dull celebration and through the many hallways until it's her leading the way, bringing us into the scullery. The lizard boy and cute pig-nosed girl gasp as we walk in.

"Names," I order, causing them to jump.

"Ryan." The boy attempts to hold his head high while shoving the blonde girl in front of him.

"Kim, your wickedness," she adds with a noticeable gulp, earning her a shoulder shove from the boy.

"I'm Shayla." The scaly girl with my hand gives me a toothy grin before turning to her friends. "She slapped the fat one." She beams with a familiar gossip that reminds me of my twin. I should be with *her* today. "In front of *everyone!*"

"Why did she hit you?" I ask with a calm I don't feel.

Shayla shrugs. "I forgot a candle."

"I'll make sure she gets it." I don't hide the malice in my promise as I take in the small room, the shelves holding buckets, cleaning soaps, and rags, with others containing hanging and dried herbs that are just what I need.

"We're used to it," Ryan explains proudly, like being able to take a punch is something to boast about.

"I'm familiar," I mutter under my breath as I pull everything I need, cross my legs on the floor, and begin grinding and stirring with precision using one of the mortar and pestles.

"You really are a witch," Shayla's astonishment beams on her darling face.

Wiping the fine dust off my fingertips, I pull the lace crown from my head and let it fall to the ground beside me.

Kim shrieks with horror, pointing to the brutal scars on the corners of my forehead. "You have—"

"Hell's crown." Shayla's sorrowful awe further confirms my suspicion about the girl; a lover of beautifully dark things because she's been tainted—*blessed* in my opinion—by the cruelty of the world.

"Go ahead." I bow my head so she can press her fingertips along the rough stitching.

"Did they hurt to cut off?"

I have to bite the inside of my cheek to keep from laughing. "How do you know I didn't slay a dreaded beast who got close enough to cut me?"

"You're a girl." Ryan rolls his eyes.

"Everyone is going to say—"

"They'll say whatever they want to as they always do," I cut off Kim's whine and pull out the vial from my bosom, uncork it, and blow into the tiny circle attached to the end. We all watch the bubbles float through the air, changing from yellow to green to orange. "You've seen me slap a horrible beast and make magic all in one night. Tell me which one you believe to be true. Did I get injured while slaying a beast, or am I the most glorious witch you've ever met who had to cut off her horns?"

Shayla giggles as I hand her the vial. Pulling the other two out of my dress, I toss them to Ryan and Kim. "But you're not a beautiful princess anymore. Aren't you angry?"

"All she has to do is eat a baby, and her skin will be perfect again," Ryan says matter-of-factly before blowing more bubbles with a wonder I don't believe he often possesses.

I brush my fingers along Shayla's scaled scars. "Hell's harsh kiss and Hell's crown are for those worthy of more than something as simple as true love's kiss or a royal diadem. It proves that even the Devil is willing to show the world the power we possess."

I knew I wanted to mark myself this way the first moment I met Shayla. Her worship of my beauty reminded me so much of Blair and the way she copies everything I do. I didn't want the little girl to strive to be me simply based on my appearance, but I also didn't want her to feel alone. If she saw a princess with scars as brutal as hers, maybe she'd stand a little taller.

It wasn't entirely unselfish. Part of me hopes that whoever bought me will see the damage and change their mind.

"They want to take yours."

A throat clears behind me, sending the kids to scurry off through the walls. I whip my head around to scold whoever interrupted me from asking Shayla what she meant, when I find Oliver's lanky form leaning into the door frame.

I grab a candle from the counter.

Just the man I was hoping to find.

Chapter Twelve

The great hall doors slam shut as I turn down the hallway. Horns blare announcing that dinner has been served. I can already picture everyone having their own pig on silver plates to celebrate the princess's royal birthday. Hordes of champagne will be passed around as speech after slurred speech will boast about the beautiful Blair and—

My thoughts and heels come to a halt. The hallway is deserted except where Hayse leans against a tight alcove near a propped-open window. His smug smirk sours when he takes me in, his hand stopping from whatever he was about to pull from his pocket.

In two swift strides, he reaches me, grips my head between his hands and tilts my chin to my chest. "Who the hell did this to you?"

Ripping his hands off me, I take a step back. "Shouldn't you be concerning yourself with what speech you're going to make about your adorable little fiancé?"

"I'm not asking again." His lips tighten.

"It would be a waste of time if you did."

His back hits the wall, leaning as he was before with a noticeable irritation and growing tension in his shoulders. "Get on your knees."

I don't get my hands to cross over my chest before he pulls them to my side and orders me again. "Either get on your knees or go back to dinner."

Either way, I'd be listening to him. I have half a mind to walk off or jump out this window to spite him, but that pull deep in my belly is throbbing too wildly to make a rash decision that would take me away from seeing this out. "Say please."

His finger brushes my cheek as he tucks a piece of hair behind my ear. "Please, wicked one, get on your knees before I bend you over this window and make you sing with the birds."

My fear of heights and the warning in his tone have me lowering to my knees in an instant, feeling the metal shift inside me as I do. I've been here before, beneath him, bowing and waiting for his next command.

Not this time.

The fullness inside me has the desperation to touch him too strong.

He stops my fingers from curling around his belt. "I didn't say touch me," he snarls. Dropping my wrists, his focus falls to the tobacco and papers he pulls from his pocket. "I just want a smoke."

"Then what do you want me down here for?"

Sticking the finished spliff between his lips, he pulls out a match, strikes it against the wall, and lifts it until smoke puffs from his mouth. He looks down at me and unlatches his pants himself. "You're going to keep it warm for me until I'm done."

As he pulls himself free, my mouth waters. I don't know what I was expecting but… I've never seen one pierced before.

"You're going to have to part your mouth a little wider than that, pretty girl."

The second I do, his fingers fall into my hair, inching me toward him. "Don't suck. Don't move. Just sit there until I'm done."

I'm about to ask why when he slides past my lips. The metal hits my teeth, cold sliding down my tongue before the heat of his skin meets the back of my throat. When he's settled, he leans back against the wall and takes another drag of the cigarette.

Forget everything that's happened in the Den. *This* is the hottest thing I've ever done. The pull between doing what I'm told to hear him call me a pretty girl again, to fucking with him so he bends me over that window is twisting at my insides in a war of good versus evil where either way I'm damned, dripping, and desperate for more.

Hale Deimos' loud, booming voice echoes in the distance, making another useless toast. The word, *glorious*, a high-pitched bellow.

My senses heighten. The sounds of laughter and Hayse inhaling the burning spliff into his lungs. The feel of the hard ground against my knees and the throbbing between my legs. The metal tightly plugged inside me.

Ash falls at my side.

Asshole. I glower and flex my throat.

He pulls back, bends down, and tugs my dress until my breasts spring free. "Do that again and I'll remove the whole damn thing." His fingers graze my nipple, and a soft whine rolls out of me. "And if you're good, I'll give you more than a taste."

He presses back in, hitting the back of my throat again before relaxing against my tongue. The quick motion and promise for more leaves saliva dripping from the corners of my mouth.

Anyone could walk by. Anyone could leave dinner and see me bent over, half-naked, with him in my mouth, but that thought doesn't scare me at all. In fact, it does the opposite. If we were in the middle of the hall instead of a cubby, it would be that much more reckless and intoxicating.

There's a rush of getting caught. A thrill that we're holding death at our fingertips just to play whatever game this is between us.

I reach between my legs, needing the friction, something, *anything*, to get this built-up tension out of me. When I glance up, he's staring down at me, his foot knocking my hand to the side. "I didn't say you could cum."

I scowl harder. This time, I hollow out my cheeks and swallow, running my tongue up his shaft until I reach that metal ball at the tip. It's bizarre that by doing what most men would beg me for, I earn myself a punishing look from him.

Click!

A door shuts around the corner. Hayse's head snaps around the alcove before dragging me closer to the window to hide us better.

"Is it all there?" My father's voice is low and deep, borderline threatening.

Hayse's hand falls to the back of my head with a slow thrust back into my mouth, his finger lifting to his lips, motioning for me to stay quiet. I can't argue or fight back unless I want to be caught, so I stay there, working my tongue up and down him as he slowly pumps in and out of me.

"Do we ever not pay?" Hale, Percival's father, asks with annoyance.

"She'll be in his chambers tonight, then. I'll ensure it."

"She better be," Hale mutters. "She's caused enough embarrassment here already, and I want to ensure she understands it's not to continue."

Hayse's fist tightens, and I can feel he's close, can feel every vein bulging the harder he becomes. His palm lands against the wall at my back as he thrusts, visibly straining himself not to make any sounds.

The second the doors close again, Hayse peers around the corner, his thrusts quickening, growing more demanding, no longer caring about the noises he makes with my mouth. "Ah fuck, you did so good." Warmth bursts down my throat and along my tongue, dripping off my lips and down my chin.

The bitter taste of him mixed with tobacco coming off his breath as he pulls me to my feet has my stomach quivering.

The door opens and closes again, but I don't care. His hands cup my breasts, this thumb flicking the piercings before sliding my dress back over my shoulders. "Happy Birthday, pretty girl."

Taking the sleeve of his shirt, he wipes my face and chin clean before nodding for me to go first.

I'm too shocked to move. Blair's birthday is only celebrated today because it's *my* actual birthday. Most false royals don't even know their real birthday because they celebrate ours as their own. It's a known tradition, and the fact that no one has bothered to wish me anything today while being overjoyed for Blair is so blatantly intentional.

"I did it to myself," I tell him, pointing to the scars on my head. "You can worry about your speech now."

Turning toward the door, I hear him call out behind me. "Sit in my seat so you can eat."

My smirk remains as high as my chin as every eye turns to me when I walk through the double doors. The whispers start the second I take my first step and grow as I take my seat beside Blair and Hayse's father, Sterling Soren, who looks me over with a mix of concern and confusion. I wince, forgetting the metal still inside of me, damning myself for not asking Hayse to take it out.

"What do you think you're doing?" King Soren sneers in my direction, his brows creasing when he notices the cuts on my forehead. I reach for wine but find a glass of water where the sweet nectar should be, forgetting Hayse doesn't drink.

Before anyone can think to take away my food, I grab my fork and take a heaping bite of the mashed potatoes. "Eating," I answer.

When Hayse enters, he strides straight toward my seat, but Raven is in it, laughing at something Percival says. He confidently takes the seat on the other side of my father, who gives him a crude glare.

"Did your horns finally come in?" Fern snickers.

"You can't sit there." Florence's voice is loud enough so half of the room's attention is solely on us. "It's not polite—"

Her wispy voice is cut off by Margarette's sputtering coughs. Peering into her glass, she pulls out a candle.

"Get a little excited with the cake?" I shove another forkful of potatoes into my mouth.

"I asked her to sit by me." Blair cuts her aunts a look before turning to me with her famous smile. "Ignore them. They mean well."

It's my turn to choke.

Blair grabs my hand gently with a questioning look that piques my interest. "I wanted to ask if you could take me back *there* tonight?"

Oh great, I corrupted the one innocent being in this entire kingdom. "I'm not sure that's a good idea."

She sighs, her brows angling in a sad puppy dog plea. "I just… I want to learn how you're so confident." Her eyes flutter to the top of my head. "Being there gave me a glimpse of what I don't have. Everyone there was so open and… fearless."

Taking her in, I notice she's no longer in that fluffy pink dress but a darling blue that nearly matches mine, except mine is off the shoulder and hers is high around her neck.

"You have to take what you want," I tell her honestly. Nothing is handed freely in this life, and if it is, it either isn't worth it or has a price that hasn't revealed itself yet. "And don't apologize for it." I stab my fork through a piece of meat and bite before sipping the champagne from her flute with a suggestive wink to further prove my point.

If I could take what I really want, I'd be back home with Eva. There hasn't been a birthday that we haven't spent together, except the year she was kidnapped.

King Hale jumps to his feet, his belly bumping the table as he stands, signally another round of toasts. King Sterling tosses back his wine, quickly refilled with their best vintage. As he raises his glass, the red sloshes over the rim, splashing onto my cheek.

A few chuckles and whispers later, I'm doing everything I can to tame that feral fiend inside of me before she makes a scene.

Sterling glances down with a smirk that says it wasn't an accident before his slurred words disgrace the entire audience.

Sliding my chair back, ensuring it makes as much noise as possible to cut the blubbering fools off, I place my hand on his arm to lower his glass and turn to address the room. "It truly is a shame a kingdom with wine as fine as the Deimos' is treated and drunk as if it were a babe's milk. They don't even let it breathe properly before they're suckling it down until they're as incoherent as one too." Gasps and whispers rise as I continue over the ringing in my ears. One laugh booms above them all— Jax, my pirate, who finishes his glass and slams it hard on the table.

"It's no coincidence their kingdom's words are *Golden and graceful, with lips so sweet you won't taste the sin 'til you sleep*, because I find myself wishing for a bed every time these two begin to talk." Quiet laughter filters through the room.

I want to stop, I really do. I'm making a fool out of not only myself but Percival, Hayse, and Blair—my father, most of all. I may have been able to hide from his grasp, but his punishments are always inevitable.

But I can't stop. It's an impulse I can't tame. "It's a true miracle Percival and Hayse aren't pompous fools or imbeciles such as their fathers."

"Hear, hear!" Jax raises his glass.

Raven raises hers and shouts, "To the prince's exalted excellencies!"

Hayse's laugh sets off a roar of uncomfortable laughter as everyone toasts and returns to their dinner with new gossip to fill their nights.

I grab the piece of bread off my plate and leave without excusing myself.

Before the door shuts, I hear the screams. "She's dead!"

Darling Devil

My Devil Doll is beautiful when she's on her knees, listening to commands with a cursing glare, looking the part with those scars on her head. She really does take what she wants, *all* of it.

I couldn't look away from her when she was kneeling on the floor, or when she gave that speech. The kings' faces would put a rose to shame with their crimson color.

She's seductive even when she's not trying to be.

But as much as I love watching her play, I'm growing impatient.

Raven survived the drugs, which means Mel has the support I don't want her to have. I want her with no one to turn to but me.

She's going to learn the hard way that no one else sees her like I do.

God Damn.

Pushing Mel's limits is impossible. Nothing I do works. I should have known having her warm me in the middle of the hall would only rile her up.

It's the eyes. It has to be. Something in them has hexed me because every plan I have goes out the window the second I look into them and find they're either glaring or giving me that *please-fuck-me* plea.

Not even hearing her father inches from us caused her a whimper of distress. There was a challenge there that pushed me to go past my limit with her.

That girl loves chaos more than I do.

And if there's anything she loves more it's making a scene.

Part of me wants to be near her every time she enters a room because no one flocks to her. They all stare and openly gawk, but no one dares to approach her, which would give me reprieve from the many who never leave me alone. I can't walk down a hallway without someone waving, or attend a feast without Blair and her aunts finding me before I've taken a breath.

The other part of me wants to be near her to never miss a moment of her chaos. Call me a fly because that black widow had me spun in whatever web she's weaved around me the second she stood from that chair and started insulting the kings.

I had to bite my lip to keep from laughing too hard.

I hate her more now than I did before. She's not supposed to be so damn alluring or *kind*. The slap she gave Margarette suggests she's the soulless, vile woman everyone talks about, but while they all turned to each other to gossip, I followed her.

I was more than thrown to find her with those children, gifting them bubbles and talking about slaying beasts, going out of her way to make Shayla feel empowered by her scales and scars. The empty place in my chest twisted at the memories of my own taunting because of my white hair and the birthmark down my chest.

Kids can be cruel over the smallest imperfections.

While everyone else fled after Margarette fell over dead, I stayed behind until the doctor confirmed it had been a heart attack. That's what they think anyway, and I'm not going to correct them because if I do, they'll hang my wicked one before I have my fun with her.

I'm pushing through her door, ready to praise and give her exactly what she's been needy for, just this once. She doesn't deserve to feel pleasure after making my life a living hell, but I need to see her face when she's in pure ecstasy, when *I'm* the reason behind it.

I haven't taken one step inside when I hear the moan, the headboard creaking against the wall, the low masculine grunts, and the sound of skin slapping together.

Percival's naked back is to me with legs wrapped around his waist as he drills into her beneath him.

I can't even be mad. This was part of the plan. She wasn't just to be my toy, but both of ours. She didn't just fuck me over when she told her father about the Deimos deals and pleasure dens, but Percival too.

CRUEL KINGDOMS

Our fathers took a page out of King Aramos' book and started using us to gain power, wealth, and alliances. Our bodies were no longer ours, but theirs.

Any *no* that I said, any scene I didn't play out, not only did I get punished, but Percival did too. They discovered they could hurt me more if they hurt him when my outburst for them to stop solidified our fate.

And it's all because Mel dragged secrets out of Percival and told her father. Percival didn't want to believe it, but as the years dragged on, he caught onto her patterns. She'd sneak away at the balls, and he'd find the men who slipped from the rooms would eventually be tied to their kingdom in new deals or alliances. Not all of them, but enough to make him see her for who she really is.

I'm *not* mad at the scene before me. Percival is her husband. He agreed to this month so I can work through my shit. It was always going to be them at the end.

That doesn't mean I can't fuck with her.

Rounding the bed, I'm ready to make my own scene, to tell him not to let her come, tell her that she's going to be punished in the morning, but the second I'm in front of them, I frown.

"Where the fuck is Mel?"

"Cellar with Oliver," Raven pants, spinning Percival so she's on top of him cuffing his hands above his head. "Be careful. She took her bow."

"Bow?" *Oliver?*

Shattering glass echoes from the back of the dark cellar. Wine bottles line the shelves along the walls and down the center aisle. A stringed instrument plays an off-tune melody that doesn't fit this dreary, clammy place.

"Come on, Mel, just a little?"

Shatter.

"I don't partake, Olly," Mel says. "I told you it doesn't affect me like it does you. You're more alert and hyper, but it makes me too tired and I pass out." I hear her pick a bottle off the shelf. "I'll stick to the wine."

"Alright, alright." The cork pops, hitting the ceiling. "She was right," he mutters under his breath. "You've always been a tease."

A low *whoosh* flies through the air. I see the arrow strike the old wine bottle, shattering it before the arrowhead ricochets off the wall.

The only other person I know who favors archery is Blair, but she's not nearly as good as Mel appears to be.

"How so?" Mel crosses the room and reaches for the fallen arrows. As she bends down, she stumbles, holding the wall to steady herself.

She drinks a lot of wine, but I've never seen her drunk.

Oliver, the scrawny twat, is at her side, *telling* her she's okay while helping her lie on the ground. "You've always sought me out at the balls, asked me to play you music, to drink with you, but you've always left with someone else."

Mel groans in response, her eyes blinking hard.

My fists ball at my side, waiting for the confirmation I need.

"Because we're *friends*."

"Are we?" Oliver tsks. "You bring me mind dusts and then make me entertain you. Then tonight, you asked me to ensure Margarette received the glass with the candle in it. I thought you finally saw me, and I wouldn't have to take your father's offer."

His fingers fumble with her laces before he gives up completely and lifts her dress.

"They said as long as I delivered you tonight, I could have you first." He laughs. *The fucker laughs* as he struggles with his pants. "Said it didn't matter because everyone's had a taste—"

Snap.

His head lifts, slowly tilting up.

My vision is black as his words gurgle with the blood that spurts from his mouth. The arrowhead is pierced straight through his throat, where I'm holding it in place.

"Everyone but you." I stare into his eyes as the life leaves him. The same way I did with the first man I was forced to let suck me off. I hate men like them, taking what isn't theirs, the entitlement…

Mel's groan pulls me from the memory, her fingers pointing at the neckline of her dress. "R-r-riiiip." Her fingers pinch at something hard embedded into the fabric. Her violet eyes latch onto mine and I'm stuck. She's the most vulnerable she's ever been, pleading me for her life, and it's a breathtaking reminder that I hold her very being in the palm of my hands. In this very moment, I could end her by simply standing still and watching her struggle until it's over.

I would never let her off so easily.

Breaking the arrowhead from Oliver's neck, I use the tip to tear at the stitching, finding a tiny vial of powder.

She takes it from me, pours it onto the back of her hand, and sniffs, lapping the leftover residue with her tongue. Her eyes widen, the purple hazel taken over by her black pupils.

"Fucking bastard!" She spits on Oliver, who's still clawing to hold the blood in his draining body. "I never thought I'd actually have to use that."

Wiping herself down, she finds her feet. Blood splatters across her face, her light hair stained pink, her cheeks dripping crimson down her chin, exactly where she had been dripping with me hours ago.

I don't know if it's the wine, the powder she inhaled, or if she's seen dead bodies before, but she's unfazed by the mess. She doesn't glance in Oliver's direction again as she takes me in, her eyes traveling every inch of me with a lick of her lips.

"You killed him." Her surprise is cute.

I nod, though it wasn't a question.

"Why?"

I had every intention of asking her what she was doing here with this man, what she was thinking being alone with someone else, but my blood is pumping with a heat that has nothing to do with the prickling fury I felt hearing and seeing her with him. "You're mine to hurt."

She steps toward me and I catch her hands before she can touch me. She's not allowed to touch me. *She*, of all people, isn't allowed to touch me.

Her frown almost makes me smile, but she doesn't let me stop her. Taking a small step back, she tugs at the laces across her chest. The pressed crease of her cleavage teasing to what I know still stings and reminds her of me with every unfortunate tug of fabric or glance in the mirror.

Her dress slips down her petite frame, pooling at her feet. The metal spikes through her taut, pink buds glimmer from the candlelight beside us.

The bastard between my legs tugs for attention—alert, ready, and throbbing to finally taste her.

Fuck it.

This time, when she takes a step forward, I let her grab the hem of my shirt, quickly taking it from her grasp and tossing it over my head. Her fingers move expertly to remove my slacks.

In sync, her legs wrap around my waist as I lift her into my arms. Her mouth parts, her tongue swiping across mine in one quick, teasing motion. My fingers fall into her silky hair while I lick and nip at her soft lips. Kissing her is the most natural thing in the world. Tobacco and blackberries, wine and dreamroot mix between us, making their own exotic flavors.

I want to hate the taste but it's the best thing next to a bitter spliff when I need an escape.

She reaches between us, gripping me with a heated groan as she lines me up and works me into her without any needed prep.

Even with how slick she is, it's not easy. She's tight, and the metal plug presses against me as I inch deeper into her, stretching her even tighter.

I was here to give her this, to give her the release she needed, but feeling her struggle to take all of me while still working her hand and hips in unison to accommodate me is fucking with my mind.

Bottles fall and shatter as her back crashes against the shelves with every inch I press into her.

Her teeth snag my lip, her head flinging back when my groin smacks against her.

I grip her ass tighter, pulling out to drive back in, hard enough to rattle the bottles, sending more falling and shattering next to us.

All I can focus on is the way she cries out, demanding more.

Women I've been with try to hide their winces under the over-the-top moans, giving me what they think I want to hear while masking their own discomfort and pain just to be the *fun* girl. Not Mel. She gives everything to me. She's bratty and submissive, and behind that cold exterior, she's warm, like a hot spring on a winter day.

She digs into my shoulder while her other hand grips the base of my neck, the same way I'm gripping hers. "You hurt so good."

Her words carve themselves into me with every thrust I carve into her. "It's because you were made for me, pretty girl. *My* perfect little toy. You're not for anyone else." I still, yanking her hair so she's staring up at me. "No one else touches you."

"Whatever you want." She returns the stinging pull at my nape, her violet eyes cutting straight through me. "But you're mine too. My punishment. My praise. My *ruin*. I don't care what you want to call it, but no one else gets you like this."

I kiss one of the scars on her forehead. "You wicked," I kiss her cheek and drive deeper into her. "Evil," *Thrust*. "Pretty Girl." I suck on her neck with the nip of my teeth. "Every inch of me is yours."

My whole soul is binding to hers with every second I spend inside her.

Her hips rock against me, pushing me even deeper. "Then fuck me like you own me."

I owned her before she knew I existed.

"You first."

She rocks again, grinding into me, singing my favorite songs while I roll her nipples beneath my thumb. They're still swollen and sore, but I can't help touching them every time I see her. Bending down, I flick my tongue over one, feeling the spikes warning.

I've never taken pleasure in being used, my name, my title, my body... none of it. But the way she's using me has me in a damn chokehold. "Hayse, please..."

"What do you want, pretty girl?"

Her hand wraps around mine, dragging it between us, using me to rub her clit. I take over, rolling soft circles as I take her harder and deeper at a steady speed that has her eyes growing heavier. Bottles shatter, glass shards pierce my feet, but all that matters is her. *Us*.

I can feel her getting closer. As she starts to throb around me, I reach around and pull out her plug, feeling her clench harder on me as I release into her, spilling so deep into her she won't be able to get me out.

We stay like this, tangled against bottles of wine, our chests unsteadying in sync, because the second I let her go, the hex that was placed on this room will break, and whatever happens next will only ruin us both.

Chapter Thirteen

"I need you to drink this." Dragon holds a clear vial toward me in the back of the cathedral. It turns out I don't burn in holy places, but it still makes my skin crawl. I can feel the hypocritical judgment growing with every second I remain here.

"I prefer not to be drugged a second time this week." Oliver's betrayal stung, but it was a necessary reminder of the masks we all wear. People pretend to be good, God-serving, and gracious. They deny ever thinking about stabbing a rival or throwing a crying baby overboard. In the end, we all show our true colors, whether it's in the face of fear, envy, lust, or greed.

I didn't toss that crying baby overboard, but I did threaten its mother on the matter.

Except for the little mice I've become fond of, children just aren't for me. They're loud and smell of constant rot. It's a blessing I'm not able to have them, honestly.

All week, the sneaky children have been leaving gifts at my door: candles, herbs, braided twine in shapes of pentagons and flowers. All gifts to give a witch out of good faith rather than ward them away out of fear. In return, I've been leaving them my own concoctions, more colored bubbles, giggle glitter, and fizzle candies.

"It's truth serum."

"You don't trust me?" I cross my arms over my '*temptress*' outfit as he calls it. I like Dragon, because he, too, doesn't hide his true feelings or thoughts. He could have lied just now, but like me, he doesn't see the point in such a frivolous choice.

"I'm not sure I trust your opinions on the truth." Cold but honest. "As fun as it's been to watch you work, the fact of the matter is, you haven't gathered anything about Hayse."

I told him everything I knew about the auction, but that wasn't enough. He wants to know *why* Hayse's name has been frequently used amongst those overseas as much as my father does. They're both convinced there's something nefarious at play.

Having nothing to hide, I take the vial from his hold and toss it back.

While we wait, he has me tell him everything again, poking for more about Jax and my connection with the pirates. I tell him Jax was a task my father sent me on to learn more about them, because he wanted a connection to a group without rules.

"Do you pride yourself in being your father's little spy?" He picks at the thick drape we're hidden behind.

"That's a tough question." I shake my head and sigh, the words tumbling out before I can stop them. "It's like asking if I enjoy jumping off a cliff when there isn't a path anywhere but down, only to find when I do make it to the bottom, I'm somehow back at the top of that damn cliff with no other option than to enjoy the freefall. If you asked if I pride myself in manipulating people by using my body to get what I need, I'd tell you no, but I've made the best of my lack of choices. Do I enjoy fucking strangers? No."

"Then why do you do it?" There's something off in the tone of his voice, like he genuinely doesn't understand. How could he? Not even I do.

"My mother died when I was young, my brother despises me, my sister… she's not always *there*. All I've had was my father. When he told me to smile, I smiled. When he told me to spin in my dress, I twirled twice, and when he told me he was proud of me, I did it all over again." My brows pinch as my lips keep moving. "But I did want to stop. He threatened to use Eva in my place, and any failure since he's given me *lessons* to ensure I never do."

He asks me about Percival and if I want to be his wife, to which I tell him I've never wanted to marry anyone but it's the life I've lived, although not conventionally yet. Percival's a good man, but I've never wanted to be chained to anyone who could tell me what to do, when and how… "except when I'm with Hayse."

My stomach turns in on itself. The cramping he left me with in my lower stomach tightens. The first three days were blissfully achy, and I can still feel him a week later. "That's not—" I can't even get the words out of my mouth.

"Tell me about your feelings toward Hayse."

I shake my head. "He's… It's nothing. He's controlling and elusive and dominating." My mind is overtaken by a rush of euphoria as a growing warmth spreads beneath my skin, wrapping around my thoughts, and coaxing out words I wish weren't there. "But I enjoy his quiet chaos as much as I enjoy seeing him struggling to keep up the façade he shows the world."

"You're too deep." He pushes off the tree. "If I told you to kill him, could you do it?"

My mouth dries at the thought. "Are you going to?"

His head cocks, studying me closer. I can't see his eyes but I can feel them. "Hayse was always going to die by the end of this."

"What?" Swallowing my shrill, I lower my voice and peek out of the curtain to ensure no one else heard. The pews are still empty. "You told me to get close so we can use him. What could he have done to deserve death? He saved me from being attacked!"

His hand collars my neck. In one quick motion, he spins me around and pushes my back against the wall. "Listen to me, temptress. You're no damsel in distress, and Hayse isn't your knight in shining armor. Hayse won't be walking down that aisle, so say your goodbyes before it's too late."

His thumb brushes my chin, knocking my head to the side with that assessing tilt in his that sends a tremor up my spine. He's a big man, tall and muscular, but aware of his own strength. He could easily pinch my neck and end me without blinking. "But understand that any man would die happy if it's at your hands, so take your pick. Either you kill him before that wedding, or I'll have to take matters into my own hands."

No.

"You want me to what?" I'm shouting, sure he can't mean what he just said.

Dragon steps back, releasing his threatening hold. The scales on his mask glimmer red from the golden sunset coming in through the stained windows. "Listen, Devil Doll, we can't let this wedding happen. Killing him is the only way. Can you do it, or are you too deep?"

I shake my head furiously. *Of course, I can do it. Hayse is a monster,* is what I want to say, what I *need* to say in order not to fail at this. But I can't, so I keep my mouth shut and smile.

"I guess we'll find out soon enough."

"Wait," I reach for him as he turns to leave. "When will I see you again?"

"If you're lucky, never."

MALICIOUS INTENTIONS

On my way back to the palace, my thoughts are a flurry of things I know and things I don't want to admit.

Dragon has it all wrong. Even if I did have feelings for Hayse, it could never happen. It doesn't matter that he saved me from Oliver. He's forbidden. He's a grave I continue to dig, and if I don't stop now, I won't have any way out but accepting a death I'm not ready for.

Blair's familiar laugh comes from up ahead. Her golden hair bounces as she skips next to Raven and Percival, all three headed toward the secret path to the Den.

I've held myself captive in Jax's room, using the last week to hide from everyone, Blair with her constant questions, my father and whatever deal he made with Oliver, and Hayse's inevitable rejection. I can't blame Blair, Raven, and Percival for growing closer, but I am a little envious to be missing out.

Jax was more than willing to let me cuddle next to him while I spent every waking hour listening for any information that could help me give Dragon what he wanted. The only thing about Hayse was someone mentioning his mother, the late Queen Leila, and how they don't believe her death was an accident, considering it was so close to the real Queen Deimos'.

I'm about to call after them when I hear faint grunts coming from behind the cathedral. My skin slicks with sweat from the blistering sun as I round the corner, quickly pulling myself back so they don't see me.

Peeking back around, I see Cain slam his fist against Hayse's ribs, his other meeting his chin and then his cheek until he's stumbling back. Hayse doesn't bother blocking the next two that strike the center of the pentagon on his stomach.

Blood drips from his lip, splitting wider when he grins at my brother. A menacing maniac is what he looks like. A man asking for the brutality my brother lives for.

Cain leaves his guard down, but Hayse doesn't take the bait. Instead, he lifts his arms behind his head. "Why'd you stop?"

My brother's shoulders rise and fall with building fury at being challenged so brazenly. "Fuck with someone else!" He spits.

His fists are fast, but he's tiring quickly. Hayse notices and starts his rebuttal, slamming his head against Cain's nose.

Hayse is taller, but not by much. His muscles are sharper and more defined, giving them a dangerous ferocity behind the black ink and dripping blood.

He doesn't let Cain take a breath before his fists fly with deadly speed on my brother's ribs.

It's the woman in the black cloak, peering around the other corner, that takes my undivided attention. Her silver hair is braided and falls down one shoulder, but it's the way it's braided that tells me exactly who she is.

I taught Dove how to braid her hair. As much as she despises me, I couldn't stand watching her struggle in that mirror.

Rounding the cathedral so no one spots me, I come up behind her. "Did Duke send you to spy on me?" That is her task in the Trove after all. She jumps, clutching her chest with a shaky breath.

Her new disguise is that of the wise women. Those who bless new births and weddings, gifting the words God speaks through them.

I've never seen her actual face, but I know she's young. It's in her round eyes and smooth hands. She hides it well, but her façade slips when something excites her, and I can't help but wonder if she's lonely. I've seen her bite her lip to keep from bursting when I mentioned Eva's love for books. She listens so intently but always leaves the table just before I think she's going to say something.

Grabbing my elbow, she pulls me into her, leaning into the side of my face to whisper. "Not everything is about you, Mel."

"Is it poisons or cures? I told you the last shipment I gave Strix was all I could give until after the wedding."

Backing away, she offers me a slight curtsy, spotting two people enjoying the gardens not far from us. She would never offer me such a gesture if she weren't undercover. We both roll our eyes as she straightens herself.

"Do *not* discuss Grim Rose in such a public place. What are you thinking?" She pinches the ridge of her nose, exasperated with me within seconds as always. "Maybe bringing you in was a mistake."

"No!" I rush out before she can think to take this from me. While I've enjoyed making different concoctions for whatever high someone is looking for, being the Grim in Grim Rose has given me a purpose, a sliver of what the Trove could give me. Dove came to me a few years ago with the idea of making dresses that help protect women after my brother told her what I could do. He's used my poisons before, reluctantly, but he still came to me for help when he needed to kill Audrey's father for abusing her all those years.

I chose *Grim* because of the lure of the forgotten kingdom that's said to be the source of the dark fairy tales' parents tell their children. It's taboo to even whisper the name *Grim* in our kingdom and I've only ever found one book that mentioned the name in our library. It held short stories that Eva loved reading to me growing up.

Dove won't discuss why she chose *Rose* but said it was a calling of sorts. She designs the dresses, I supply the fabric and whatever draught she needs, and Strix makes them a reality. I have my suspicions she's brought Audrey in to create them as well. That woman is brilliant with a needle and now has any fabric at her fingertips.

"Since you're here," my intuition hasn't steered me wrong yet, and with Dove showing up, it's all the sign I need to grasp this opportunity, "could you look into someone for me?"

"Hefty price, considering it's for you."

"I would expect nothing less." I lean closer into her neck, nipping her lobe to mess with her. "Find what you can about Percival Deimos and Hayse Soren's mothers."

Her head jerks back to see if I'm serious. "They died."

"And that's not odd? If real royalty dies, do the false ones too? Or was this a one-off coincidence?"

Her neck dips with a contemplating look on her withered face. "Even the dead aren't useless." Her quote gives me pause. I haven't heard that since I was a child. A saying, an old one, but one that always made me frightful and is eliciting memories I would rather never think of again.

"What's your price?"

She shakes her head. "I'll call on you when I need it, but if I do find what you're looking for, it's double."

Her eyes widen and before I can look behind me, my scalp screams as my head is ripped back. "Have you been avoiding me, wicked one?"

My pulse climbs to where Hayse's fist pulls at my hair. He orders Dove to give him her cloak and drapes it over me before tossing me over his shoulder too fast for me to fight. Without being able to see where we're going, I keep my voice down to not be caught in such a precarious position.

"We're in public!" I pinch his side.

"Thinking you could hide from me was your first mistake. The other was licking that old hag's ear."

As my senses fill with copper from the blood and sweat that coats him, I hear footsteps of people passing us and him explaining that he's taking a prisoner to the kings.

The summer breeze halts and I know we're inside. Turn after turn, he continues, until a door opens and slams shut. A lock *clicks* into place.

I'm ready for him to put me down, but the sound of dragging stone grates my ears before he takes a few steps, and it grates again, the muscles along his back working to move whatever it is.

My body flings down, meeting a soft mattress. I toss the cloak off me, finding that I can't see anything. I can only make out the faint outline of his body moving to light the sconces, turning the pitch-black room into an amber haze. With the tiniest bit of light, I can see the walls are gray without any windows. Swords, daggers, and shields hang on display. A long wooden table takes up an entire wall, layered in tools, half of which I've never seen. There's a bowl of tobacco, dreamroot, and thin paper on the nightstand. The air smells of a burning hearth.

"Where are we?"

"Some place no one will hear you." I can hear the smile in his voice without having to look at him.

He takes my hand and pulls me to my knees, spinning me around to untie the strings on the back of my dress. His fingers are fast, moving down my spine, loosening the snug fabric and slipping it off my shoulders. His chin grazes my ear. "Tell me, in the last week, did anyone else see you like this?"

His fingers move with the fabric, slithering down my breasts, not stopping when they free over the neckline. He continues, trailing over my navel, my scar, until he's cupping my center. Just when I think he's going to pause, I'm gasping into his mouth as his fingers press into me. "Answer me."

"No!" I comply through a groan when he adds another.

"Then where were you?" He removes his fingers to drag me to my feet, the dress falling to the floor before he spins me to face him.

My body melts for him, my mind a mush of compliance. Being without him has only increased my need to do whatever it takes to be with him again.

More blood drips down the cut in his raised brow.

"One of the guest rooms."

"They're all occupied, so either you're lying about no one else seeing you this way or you're lying about where you were."

I glarc up at him. "I'm not lying at all."

With the truth serum still fresh in my system, I couldn't if I wanted to.

"Then why have you been avoiding me, wicked one?"

My chest is heavy and I have to bite my tongue to hold the words I refuse to say out loud. Words that physically hurt my head not to release. When his thumb brushes my lip, they tumble out anyway.

"Because I'm too fucking deep." My hands fall to his waist to steady myself. "I hate whatever this is because it can't happen. It doesn't matter that I..." I don't. I can't, but as he continues studying me with that hateful glare, I know I can't leave him alone either. "It can only be physical."

"Just physical," he repeats.

Before it can be anything more than that, he *lets* me lift his shirt, rising to my toes to pull it over his head before I move to unlatch his pants. He watches me undress him at my own steady pace.

I can't look anywhere else but his beautiful, inked body, all three piercings making my thighs clench. His fingers lift my chin to meet his growing smirk. "But you're going to beg me this time."

I lift back onto my toes and bring his neck to my lips, grazing my teeth along his pebbled flesh where the vein thumps violently. "I hid from you." My hand slithers around his ribs while the other wraps around his length between us. "Mistake number one."

His groan rattles my chest as I stroke him once. Twice. The third time, he brings my hands behind my back, twisting me to get the position he wants. "Rules."

"Greenfire. Three taps. Breathe." I tell him, biting down the trickle of panic when I see him grab the rope off the table and quickly restrain my hands behind my back. It's tight enough that I push my chest out more to release some of the pressure.

He lowers me to the floor, until my knees are spread apart with my cheek against the thick, rich rug, and my ass in the air.

His thighs brush the back of mine, his length moving up and down my slick center.

Smack!

His hand comes down on my flesh, rocking me forward, pressing my cheek harder into the floor. "Count."

"One," I yelp as another hand finds new sensitive skin. "Two." I count every single strike, but it's the feel of his cock rubbing against me that's the real torture. "Twelve. Hayse, please…"

"Please, what?" His finger curls inside me, pumping in and out before moving toward my back entrance.

"Fuck me, *please* fuck me."

All breath is ripped from my lungs as he slams inside of me, driving in and out, over and over without stopping. He's fast and ruthless and everything I need. His finger works my backside in the same rhythm as his free hand grips my hair, pushing me harder into her rug.

"Let me go." I'm building so fast, but I need more. I'm throbbing in all the right places. "I can't cum like this," I say quickly before the shame can settle over me. I've always found sex pleasurable, but I'm not one of those girls who can finish by penetration alone. It usually takes my own fingers. I prefer mine over others because I know exactly where I need them.

But he doesn't let me go. He reaches around, keeping one hand on my hip with a grip tight enough to bruise while the other works my center, circling that needy nub. His fingers are so delicate and slow, deliberate, as he continues to pound into me like he hates me.

My vision is solid black with my release, as if I'm drowning in the damnation that resides behind his eyes. I clench around him, my nipples rubbing against the rug, the sensitive sting dragging me out even longer.

His finger is at my backside again. As he works a second and third finger into me, he reminds me to breathe. I don't know how I manage when I feel so full. "That's it, pretty girl, you're about to be mine in every way." He pumps in and out, coaxing soft whimpers from me. "Isn't that what you want?"

"*Umph*. Y—yes."

His piercing presses against me, replacing his fingers, stretching me wider, inch by agonizing inch. I follow his instructions to breathe until his groin slaps against me. He grips my hips as he retreats, slowly sliding back into me, letting me get used to him.

"*Hayse*..." I let out a strained breath. "I licked that old crone's ear." I wiggle my ass. "Mistake number two."

"*Fuck*. That's right."

Smack!

His palm comes down hard on me. Tears swell in my eyes at the sting, mixing with the pressure. He pulls out and slams back into me with another *smack*, again and again, bringing my hips back to meet him.

As my vision blurs this time, my hair is pulled back so it's his black eyes I'm lost in. His tongue dips into my mouth as he stiffens, spilling inside me.

It's the way he stays inside me, the way he kisses me deep and savoringly, that scared me the first time. This time, I'm doomed. I don't want to leave this—*him*.

I'm so sore and out of it. I close my eyes, feeling cold and empty when his weight lifts and he's no longer there. When the ropes snap away, my shoulders cry out in relief.

He tosses the knife on the nightstand and picks me up, lying me on the bed. "Where are you going?"

He turns back, a step away from the mattress. "I need to clean you up."

"No." I grab his hand and pull him next to me. "I don't care about the mess. Don't leave me."

Please don't leave me. My heart rate spikes, remembering all the times I was left behind to be forgotten.

His face falls but he doesn't argue. Falling next to me, he wraps his arm around my shoulder with the other tugging my waist against him.

We don't talk. We don't need to.

He tenses, but lets me trace his tattoos, following the random patterns, the smoke, the skulls, all of it. "Did you design these?" I saw his notebooks and canvases, it wouldn't surprise me if he drew his own tattoos.

"Mhm. I tattooed most of them myself."

"Can you tattoo me?"

His head lowers, the knot between his brows twitching with surprise. "What do you want?"

I shrug. "Surprise me."

"I have everything here if you're serious."

"I am."

"Alright." His arm drapes over me enough to reach the scar along my abdomen. "Tell me about this first."

I swallow. Usually, I tell people it was an accident, or someone kidnapped me and took my organs for the black market, but that doesn't seem so funny anymore. "My extracurricular activities would have led to unwanted results my father didn't care for."

His jaw tightens. "I'm not a fucking idiot. Are you saying your father made it so you can't have children?"

"Not before he took the one in it." I pull my hand from his and sit up, leaning against the wall to angle away from the sharp ache in my ass. I wrap the sheet tighter around me just to hold onto something. "I don't know why I told you that. That's... You can't tell anyone. Swear you won't tell anyone."

He sits up, leaning over his knee with a scowl I don't believe is for me.

"I don't want them anyway," I continue to ramble before he can say anything. "They smell awful and take all your time away from—"

"Why would he do that?"

"Please don't ask me questions," I plead, grabbing his hand in desperation. "I can't lie to you right now."

"Then don't." He flips his hands so his is on top of mine. "Why the fuck would he do that to you?"

Truth serum or not, I want to tell him. After telling Cain about our father, it felt like we got past something I didn't know was between us.

"He has these episodes every few years where he isn't okay. When he's far into them, he thinks I'm my mother. He found out Percival and I were together, and when it was obvious I was pregnant, he thought I was my mother with another lover's baby inside me. So, he took it out.

Only, the woman he had oversee the surgery ordered everything to be removed. She said he demanded it because he had enough heirs and wanted to ensure this never happened again."

It's fascinating how most women go through what everyone calls the *Triple Goddess*, the ultimate witch—maiden, mother, crone. And yet it's me who they claim is the mistress of all evil, the title of witch, when I'm unable to be a mother, and I likely won't live long enough to be a crone.

"When he understood what he had done," I continue, unable to keep a single secret at bay, "he said it would be easier for me to seduce secrets since I don't have anything that prevents me from doing what's needed."

"Does Percival know?"

"Not about the baby, but I told him I couldn't have children. I didn't want him blindsided."

His eyes narrow on me as if he's trying to work through something. "He could have sold you out and called off the entire marriage because of it. You trusted that secret with him?"

"I think part of me was hoping he would, so we could get out of it, but I think he saw the benefit of someone like me at his side. I'll let him be with whoever he wants."

"He's an idiot," he growls, caressing my cheek and pressing his lips against mine. It's the softest he's ever kissed me. "I'm sorry that happened to you." He moves down my neck. "All of it." His lips trail along my collarbone, pushing me back to settle his torso between my legs, kissing down my navel, over my scar…

Before he can move any lower, I sit up and pull his face back to mine. "What's the ring for?" I tug at the amethyst on his pinky, quickly changing the subject.

"That's your question?" His brow rises, his lips threatening a laugh. "Why? Do you want it?"

My smile tugs higher. "You already gave me two pieces of jewelry, if you give me anymore, I might think you like me."

His smile drops, an understanding settling over his features. "Just physical, wicked one."

Hayse

It's well past my training schedule, but lying next to Mel, my mind isn't racing as it usually is. It can't with her talking in her sleep, whimpering about having to kill me. It makes sense, I just spent the last eight hours putting a needle and ink to her skin, fucking every one of her holes, feeding her blackberries and water, cleaning her up, and not necessarily in that order.

Needless to say, she's exhausted and wanting to kill me is perfectly reasonable.

Which is how I felt after she wouldn't let me put my tongue between her legs. I'm positive it's payback in some way. She even used her safe word, *greenfire*, when I tried again, saying it was too intimate.

My dick was in her mouth an hour ago, so her logic is as wild as she is.

I settled for using my fingers, but I can't deny that tasting her has been my sole thought since she turned me away.

Just like I can't stop needing to prove her wrong and make her cum from penetration. It makes so much sense why edging her didn't lead to her begging me to give her the relief she needed. She's used to doing it herself.

Not anymore.

The temptation to use the shackles and force my face between her legs almost got me. She thinks they're for sex, but she couldn't be more wrong—not entirely. I'll use them on her now, but they're there to keep me from hurting myself in my sleep. I don't just walk when I'm unconscious, I'm violent. I once woke up in the middle of stabbing my own thigh. The night terrors don't just feel real, they are real for me.

But her… I enjoy tying her up, making her my own perfect, obedient little nightmare.

I hate that I could have been doing this all week. I would have found her sooner if I wasn't busy trying to figure out who in the fuck bought her in the auction. Percival and I have both talked to every single guest and came out empty-handed. We're down a few because I couldn't keep my shit together when they sneered her name with insults. Names she's too familiar with but shouldn't be—wicked, evil, witch… She's *mine* to fuck with.

I stroke her cheek where she's resting on my chest, admiring the new art that takes up half of her back. She said to surprise her without any other instructions, and I might have gotten carried away.

I always get carried away when I'm focused on creating something new.

I offered to get her alcohol or something else for the pain, but she looked at me as if I thought she was a child and told me to get to work.

"*Mmm*… I'm hungry." She yawns, her silver-blonde hair splayed over me like a blanket. "Did you finish?"

"Many times." I chuckle, pressing a blackberry to her lips. She takes it with the cutest giggle. How can that mouth say the most depraved, wonderful things my ears have ever heard, the sweetest songs that pierce straight through me, and then giggle like that? As if she wasn't begging to swallow me an hour ago. "The outline's done, but I wasn't able to shade it all in yet."

"Well, I'll make coffee and pancakes, and then you can finish."

"You can cook?" I watch her struggle to stand, her knees buckling.

"You'd be surprised what I can throw together." She winks and looks around, realizing there aren't any doors here. "I'm not going to lie, I can't cook, but I was going to try if I could find my way out of here."

"I'm not letting you out like that." I make a point to keep myself relaxed, my arm resting behind my head, my ankles crossed, while reaching for my dagger and twirling it between my fingers. My eyes start at her ankles and rake up to her knees, thighs, and the diamond peak at the top of her legs. Red welts cover every inch of her round ass. Her back is a peachy tone except for the new black ink along the side. The arch at the base of her spine deepens as she presses her hands against the wall in an attempt to push it open.

"The maids could be out there, so unless you want their deaths on your hands, you're going to want to cover up before I let you out."

She turns back, crossing her arms.

I hate it. I don't know why, but every time she does it, I want to yank them apart so she stops hiding herself from me. It's her form of a mask. She shows the world who she is, but the second she crosses her arms, she's putting up a wall. A wall I'll tear down every chance I get.

It has me jumping to my feet and stalking over to her to do just that as I drag the sheet with me and throw it over her shoulders. "You're *my* toy, remember? Not another man, or woman, is allowed to see or touch you again. Not Percival either. Just me, pretty girl."

The violets in her eyes sparkle a little darker every time I call her my pretty girl. "Has anyone ever said you don't play nicely with your toys?"

"No one's been able to handle how well I play, so no." I pull the sheets tighter around her shoulders. "Pancakes and coffee." My lips graze her cheek as she turns away from me and I smack her ass, making her yelp with another giggle.

Grabbing the edge of the protruding stone, I drag the tight opening, letting her through first. She looks back, seeing that we emerged from the fireplace in the corner of my chambers.

I tell her to be quick in the washroom while I slip into pants. I'm tempted to follow her, take my time with her in the tub, but I'm too eager to see how she manages to throw together pancakes and coffee after she admitted she can't cook.

It's not just physical.

It's damning.

A knock comes from the door. Knowing it's probably Percival, I open it without thinking twice.

I'm pushed back as legs wrap around my waist.

"Did you hear the good news?" I'm too in shock that Blair is touching me to care what she's saying. No one touches me, not outside of those fucking rooms. Not unless I'm in control. I'm peeling her arms from around my neck when she brings her lips against mine. "They moved up the wedding. We're getting married in two days!"

Glass shatters.

Mel emerges from the washroom in a robe tightly wrapped around her and a towel in her hair. "Thank you for letting me use your bath since mine was broken." She tries to hide it, but I spot the blood dripping from her knuckles before she closes the door between us.

Chapter Fourteen

Air won't hit the bottom of my lungs as I struggle to breathe in and out at a rapid pace.

Hayse and Blair were always going to marry. Seeing her wrap her arms around him shouldn't have been a problem. Seeing her kiss him is what pushed me over. And when she said they were to marry in two days, all I saw was red. Literally, my hand was covered in it.

Impulsive violence isn't something I'm familiar with. I don't even remember smashing the mirror with my fist, but the evidence is here, dripping off my knuckles.

I didn't wait to stick around and watch them fuck their happiness. I ran out of there so fast I didn't care who saw me leaving his room in only a robe.

Fortunately, the hall is empty, except for Raven, whose smile falls the moment she spots me hyperventilating. "Mel," her voice drops an octave, telling me she already knows. "I'm so sorry." She catches up to me while I continue with a determination to get as far away from him as possible. There isn't an inch of me that isn't sore, an itching reminded of his touch.

Walking over a tightrope in six-inch heels would be easier than this.

"If you need a distraction, let me help. I can grab Percival if you need him." She grabs my arm, spinning me around to face her. "Just tell me what you need. Anything."

"A case of vintage and something to ruin." Like Hayse's canvases or Blair's pretty dresses. What I really need is my serenade snuff; anything that will numb me from this feeling in my chest. I don't share my feelings. I don't typically dwell on them, so talking won't help.

We pass Jax down the hallway, who clocks how fast we're moving and does a double take. He calls after me, asking what's wrong, but I wave him off with a quick flick of my wrist.

"Give me an hour. I promise I'll find something that will help." Raven rushes back, leaving me to drown in the billowing reality crashing down on me like a winter storm.

I step into my room, ready to fall against the door behind me, but it slams before I get a chance.

"You disappoint me."

"No. No, Daddy, please. *Please!*" I haven't begged this hard since I was a young teen and thought it might do something, but as I brace myself against the wall, my leg chained at the edge of the tallest tower, a foot away from the vast open sky, I beg for my life.

The white jacket secures my arms tightly around my chest.

My father's disappointment stares back at me without an ounce of mercy. "You found nothing on Hayse or why the overseas royalty has been favoring him. You made a fool of me and the kings. You disappeared for days. You know exactly what led you here." He pulls the mask from behind his back. "And you know why I must do this."

"No. Please, daddy. *Please.* If you leave, you'll forget me again! I can't—"

Smack!

His palm slams across my face. I'm so thrown, so panicked by the height we're at that I forget to overexaggerate and lean into the strike to stop most of the impact.

"Don't worry, Rosebud." His meaty palms cup my cheeks as a tremor takes hold of my body. He only ever called my mother Rosebud. If he thinks I'm her again, his episode is already too far. "You're going to have visitors, so if I do forget you, someone else will know you're here. Now, be my good girl and open."

Smack!

His palm strikes me so hard I fall to my knees, my temple taking the impact without my hands to stop me. He bends down, forces my jaw open, and places the tongue retainer around my head, the mask digging into my lips to keep them apart as the springs hold my tongue in place.

Hot tears run down my cheeks.

It's not the height I'm thinking about, how I'm inches from one wrong turn that could lead to my fallen death. It's not about being forgotten, failing my task, or not making it into the Trove.

All I can think about is how Dragon promised to kill Hayse if I don't. If I don't find a way out of here, Hayse is going to die.

I searched for Mel in her chambers, every guest room, the cellars, the great hall, circled back to my chambers, Percival's… I can't find her anywhere.

I don't know what I'm going to say or do, I just know that I need to find her. The look in her eyes when she left made me shudder. They weren't fiery or determined to right a wrong, they were like mine—empty.

I've resorted to searching places she wouldn't normally go, the stables, the cathedral… On my way to the library, my father and King Hale round the corner, headed straight toward me.

"Have you seen Mel?" I ask, leaving no stone unturned.

Hale nods his head for me to follow them to the nearest room, ordering the man occupying it to find himself someplace else. "You've had your fun." My father closes the door. "It's time to end it with that witch."

I clench my fists, a habit when I hear that term refer to her with that sneering tone. "There's nothing to end."

How in the hell did they know about Mel? We were never public, and the Forbidden Den has always been safe from their eyes, or so I thought.

"Good," Hale says sternly, "because we're taking out King Aramos at the wedding. His son, Cain, has already shown that he doesn't care to rule, which means Mel would have a decent claim to the throne, more so with our backing."

"*You* want her on the throne?" These two have despised her more than I have, hating her brash, boldness.

"She's married to my son, so yes. He'll rule their kingdom. This has always been the plan."

As much as I don't want to reveal how much I know about their auction, I need to know. "If that's the case, why auction her off? Who bought her?" I've always known I was being auctioned off, but I never considered that others were, that *she* was.

The kings exchange glances with something close to disappointment laced with a decision. "Come with us."

I follow them across the palace, into the abandoned wing, and up the spiraling tower. I hate this place. They used to bring me here when I 'acted out' by defying them.

The hairs on my neck rise with every step.

When we reach the top, Hale unlocks the door with the rusted key. A warm gust of wind passes as we step through. I don't make it another step before my wrists are shackled and tugged back against the wall.

That's not what I'm focused on.

I'm only aware I can't move because the second I understand what I'm looking at, I do everything in my power to run toward her.

My wrists wail, the stone loudly cracks with the force I use to throw myself forward.

The purple in Mel's eyes isn't calming right now, not with the way they're red and dripping tears. Her body is sprawled on the floor, as far away as she can get from where her foot is shackled to the edge that is wide open to the night sky. Her arms are trapped in the straitjacket, and the mask on her face is holding her mouth wide open with her tongue held in place.

I've dreamt of this day, of her wearing the tongue retainer, the device I created, specifically with her in mind. I was young and full of the need to inflict as much pain as possible. I only lived for vengeance. It's all that flowed through my veins.

Seeing it used on her now…

"It's nothing she isn't used to, boy." Hale steps before me, knowing the exact distance to stay out of my reach. "Her father is punishing her for disappearing on us." His grin, the way his double chins dimple with it, makes me sick. "You asked who bought her. We did."

Crack!

The cane whips across my abs. It doesn't hurt the way they want it to, but I grunt so they believe it does. I stopped feeling their abuse years ago. It's their words that have my heart beating in my ears.

"I overheard your plans for her." My father speaks up with the cane loose in his palm. "It gave us the idea to punish her thoroughly, so she understands her role as queen. To be *quiet* and obedient and stop causing so many damn scenes."

"But a little birdy told us what's been going on in the Den. That you favor her a little too much. So, we moved up the wedding before you could get any ideas about running off," Hale continues with a pudgy smirk. "We agreed to give you tonight to understand that we have the means to keep her in this state anytime we want, not that you needed the reminder. If she doesn't learn her lesson tonight, we'll ensure she learns it tomorrow, *after* the wedding. Do you understand?"

They don't let me say anything before my father whips the cane across my cheek. That one hurt. I can feel the blood dripping down my neck. "Don't think we bought her for nothing, boy."

My father nods for Hale to leave, telling him he needs one last word alone. This man is dead to me. Whatever he has to say means nothing.

"I know you well enough to know that you never intended to go through with this wedding." He grabs my chin between his fingers, looking at me with a seriousness he never has before. "But don't get any ideas, do you hear me? Even if it were possible, you two could never happen."

He tosses my chin to the side. "Hale is determined to mentally and physically break her. Despises her for manipulating Percival and telling her father about the overseas deals and Dens. It forced him to ally with Aramos and marry his only heir to the prick's witch daughter. Do keep in mind that she is already married to him—your best friend and double." He pauses, brows knitting at the growl that rumbles through my chest and has the nerve to point at her. "Look at her, son. This isn't a start to what he plans for her, what *I'll* do to her, you, Percival, that little friend Raven Percival has grown fond of. They'll all suffer if you don't go through with the wedding to Blair. You don't understand what's at stake if you don't."

He looks back at Mel one last time before making for the exit. "Say your goodbyes. We'll get you in the morning, but she stays until after the wedding to ensure you do as you're told."

The moment the door slams shut, I'm yanking my body, tugging and pulling at the chains, but all I'm doing is tiring myself out. "Mel!" I call out. "Mel, look at me."

Her head burrows further into the floor, tucking her chin to her chest. "God dammit, Mel." My voice is too harsh, but I hate that I can't do anything to help her. I've never felt more trapped, more paralyzed, more fucking useless than I do right now. "Please, just look at me, pretty girl."

Her head angles just enough to look up at me. "There, see. That wasn't so hard."

It probably was. That mask is heavy to add to the torment and is the reason she's lying on the floor like that. "Blink once for yes and twice for no. Do you understand?"

One blink.

"Are you okay?" No, she's not. Her eyes are heavy from exhaustion, and it's not just from being tied up. I spent all night using her body, marking her with ink. She *might* have slept for an hour, not to mention she's hardly eaten anything but wine since she's been here.

One blink.

"Are you lying?"

One blink and a sniffle. Fresh tears form, racing down her cheeks. Drool drips from her lips onto the floor.

I have too many questions. Is she in pain? Did her father hurt her? Did anyone else visit her before we came in? From this angle, I can see the length of her legs with no hint at a dress or slip.

"Do you want to sleep it off?"

Her eyes angle, softening in a way that tells me she heard everything my father said. Two blinks.

"Okay, then I'm going to talk to you all night, and if you fall asleep, that's okay." My chains don't allow me to sit or kneel, giving just enough room to make me think I can, but pulls at my wrists if I try. Resting my back against the wall, I cross my ankles, pretending we're back in the hall outside dinner when I stood in this same position waiting for her to find me.

"We can start with your tattoo. You talk in your sleep. There was a lot about a dragon, and it made me think of you; how terrifying and divine you both are, how you burn with a fire that only an ancient mythological creature would because you weren't meant for a world as boring as this one." I smile, remembering the exact image that came to mind when she asked me to ink her. "It's a long black dragon that runs down the side of your back. Its head peeks above your shoulder, and its tail curls at the other side of your hip."

Her eyes crinkle like she wants to smile.

I turn my wrists, lifting my pinky. "You asked about the ring. I made it. It was the first thing I made with the thought of getting out of this life."

I ramble on about everything and nothing. I tell her I can't cook to save my life, but I can draw, and like her, I can make something out of nothing because I can't stand the thought of sitting still—except when I'm with her. I can sit in her silence and feel content. I don't tell her that last part.

All this leads me to wish I could ask her questions right back. I want to know everything about her. I chose to ignore anything to do with her because I didn't want to ruin the horrific image I had, the seducing, whispering, wicked witch who ruined my life.

We're like this for hours. My thighs burn, my arms ache from the weight of the chains, my mouth tastes of blood, but I don't stop talking for a second.

Just as I open my mouth to tell her more, the door bursts open.

Mel's eyes widen, her head lifting from the ground as Jax storms in with three children behind him. I made sure to know who he was after he laughed at her speech on her birthday. He's the one guest I couldn't find to ask about the auction and part of me thought that maybe he bought her, until another pirate laughed in my face and said he couldn't afford a plate of food let alone a woman.

Jax rushes to Mel's side, delicately removing the tongue retainer from her face and pulling a key to unlock her shackles. Her legs flail as she lifts to her knees and stumbles straight into me, knocking me back against the wall.

As the kids work to remove my restraints, all I can do is tuck my chin into the top of her head.

Once one hand is free, I wrap it around her, yanking the ties behind her back. She yelps in pain as the straitjacket falls off, her arms probably sore from being stuck in that position for hours.

Jax removes his top and slips it over her shoulder. He's a thin guy, but she's so small, the thing drapes to her knees.

"How did you know?" The possessive side of me wants to rip his shirt off her and use mine, but now isn't the time. When the boy finally frees my other hand, I lift her into my arms and we all descend the stairs.

"The thing about pirates is we know how to hide and we know how to find the rats." He winks at the children and explains how he knew she was in trouble the moment he saw her walking down the hallway looking as if someone murdered her entire family before her eyes. Apparently, if a night passed where she didn't check in with him, he promised to find her to knock some sense back into her. Do I like that she trusts a sleazy pirate or that she's been cuddled up to him all week? *Absolutely fucking not.* But considering he just saved her when I couldn't, I won't be laying a hand on him.

"There's an abandoned cottage in the forest. The old cook died last year, and we've been sneaking to it every week. No one else knows about it. The kings..." The blonde girl with an upturned nose pauses. "They mean to hurt her really bad, but she can stay there. She'll be safe."

Taking the back exit, the kids give me detailed instructions on how to find the place.

It takes a while, but I keep her talking, asking all the questions that I wanted to in that room. She's so exhausted, I don't think she knows she's answering them. Her favorite color is black, and she's been obsessed with blackberries since someone threw them at her. A piano being played is the happiest sound, but only when it's a sad cadence. She hates singing because she hates someone thinking so highly of themselves, which only makes me laugh. The black ring on her finger was from someone special long ago. Not a lover, but someone who saw her when no one else did.

By the time I'm kicking open the cottage door, shaking out the covers, and lying her against me on the small bed, the sun is rising.

A tremble runs through her as she begs, deep in sleep, "...plea... don't forget me. *Please.*"

"Impossible."

Holding her tighter, a new feeling sparks, something I never thought I'd ever feel. It's been slowly eating me from the inside since she's been here. It's not something I can keep. *She's* not something I can keep.

Seeing her lying in that torture room put everything into perspective. This is my fault. If I hadn't come up with the idea to use her, the kings wouldn't have overheard me, they wouldn't have bought her for their own revenge. She wouldn't have ended up in that room.

If I hadn't created that tongue retainer, it never would have been used on her.

There's no running; my face is too prominent just as much as her reputation is, to the public, royalty, and overseas.

The plans have twisted a bit but it hasn't changed. When I'm gone, she'll be at Percival's side, where she was always meant to be. Loathing me so fiercely, she'll love him that much more.

He's the best man I know and will take care of her, not that she needs him. And once I take care of the kings, they'll have nothing in their way.

My lips brush her forehead. "I'm sorry, pretty girl."

Chapter Fifteen

"This isn't a good idea. She lo—"

"I know. It's for the best. Are you going to help me or not?"

Every inch of me is sore when I open my eyes. My back is on fire and too sensitive from the ink needled into it, my lower stomach is cramping, and my ass aches from Hayse brutal thrusts and punishing palm. My shoulders burn, and my jaw feels as if someone tried to rip it from my face.

I gather the faintest scent of tobacco and blackberries, but when I open my eyes, Hayse isn't here. I'm in a room I don't know, smaller than the guest rooms in the palace.

The shutters are closed, but I can tell it's midday.

I find my way to the tiny kitchen, gasping when I see Raven trying to work the spinning wheel in the corner. "Oh, thank all the sweet peaches!" She jumps and rushes toward me. "I don't know what the hell that thing is, but it doesn't work." She hands me a water and a bowl of oats. "How are you feeling? Hayse said—"

"Where is he?"

"He's..." Her mouth opens to say something, hesitating for too long before sighing. "He's at the Forbidden Den."

I'm out the door in seconds. My head jerks in every direction, taking in the unfamiliar surroundings until I spot the mountain in the distance.

"Hold on! I'll take you!"

I let her catch up to lead the way. I'm listening but not fully while she fills the quiet with chatter about Blair, how she's not as posh as she expected but similar to us when she isn't acting shy. She talks about Percival being a heathen and how much she has in common with him. I could have laughed if my stomach wasn't knotted with anxiety. Raven and Percival are the same in so many ways: loyal, naturally motherly, and unable to pronounce the word *no*. Not to mention their vigorous appetites. Raven is unashamed of being a harlot and Percival would never apologize for his needs.

The pit in my stomach deepens the closer we get.

My intuition is telling me that something is wrong.

The mountain isn't too far, but it takes us the rest of the day through the forest and along the river.

The Den is busier than usual, probably because weddings put people in a strange mindset, either stressing about their own impending marriage or trying to find someone to be the other half in the one they've dreamed of.

It doesn't matter how many people are here, I find Hayse the moment I step in. He's leaning down to nuzzle someone's neck with that golden staff in his hand, pulling her toward the backroom.

He doesn't bother closing the door behind him.

Raven is at my side, pulling my arm, begging me to turn back and leave.

I can't.

I can't hear her. No one else exists as I watch Blair turn to face him. His hands come up quick to stop her from touching him, muttering orders I can't hear but know as she falls to her knees. He jerks back a step when she reaches for him again.

What knocks the wind from me is when he takes a step forward and lets her grip his thighs. The moment she does, his head turns and his soulless eyes latch onto mine with every step he takes to walk around to face her back.

On the first tap against her ass, his tight grin lifts.

Raven tries to stop me again, but I'm already across the Den, down the hallway, and in the room, ripping the cane from his hands before she gets a complete sentence out. "What are you doing?"

"Playing with my soon-to-be wife. Why don't you find your husband?"

"But—"

"We had fun, Mel. But it was just physical, remember? You were my toy, and I have a new one."

"Hayse—" My voice cracks. I don't know what I expected, but after the last two nights, I convinced myself that this was different. That *he* was different.

"I needed someone tried and true. And you didn't disappoint." His chuckle fills with sadistic malice. "You bad girls are a good time, but no one could actually love someone like you." My chin lifts by the press of his knuckle, scolded by the belittling sneer he casts down his nose. "I pity Percival for having to be tied to you." He leans into my ear, his breath hot and still sends a shiver down my spine. "At least when you die, he'll never have a reminder."

That burn in the pit of my stomach flares when he grazes my scar. My teeth are on the verge of cracking to keep the thickening ball in the back of my throat.

Greenfire. Greenfire, greenfire, greenfire. If there was ever a time to say it, it's now. I hate him. But this man could light the kindling that kills me, and I'd tighten my lips before I ever admit defeat to him.

"I know." I manage to say through clenched teeth. Swallowing my pride, I pull away from his scorching touch and start for the door.

The thing is, I made peace with who I am long ago, and while every part of me wants to crumble because it's *him* who's taking a sledgehammer to the tatters of my soul, I grip the doorframe and twirl back around.

"But don't feel too bad for him." I let the smirk, the sinister mask, fall perfectly on my face. "Like you said, we bad girls are a good time." I wink and leave them to search for my husband.

It doesn't take long to spot Percival. He's on Hayse's usual chaise, watching Raven in the corner with another man and woman. It's the closest thing to a scowl I've ever seen on him.

Starting at his feet, I crawl over him with a sway in my naked hips until I'm straddling his waist. "I need a favor."

His grin matches mine. "As do I, Mi Vera." His warm palms slither over my curves to lift the hem of the tunic over my head and toss it to the side. Rising to his elbows, he brings my nipples into his mouth one at a time.

My head falls back with a sultry groan at how sensitive they've become since the piercings.

His tan chest is warm under my palms where they slide down every hard ripple of muscle until I'm at his waistband.

"Look at *him.*"

I shake my head.

"Trust me."

I do, only to find Hayse standing by a bent-over Blair. His hand is tight on the golden cane, but my whole focus is on his eyes as I crawl back to lower myself down Percival, dragging my tongue and sucking kisses down his toned stomach. As I pull him free of the briefs, I hesitate.

I hate Hayse's words. I *am* tried and true to be a good time, but I never felt that way with him, not until now. If that's what he thinks of me, I'll show him exactly how right he is by doing what I always do, by become what they expect so it doesn't hurt.

My lips run over Percival, base to tip, my tongue darting out once I get to his crown, never taking my eyes from Hayse.

I can see Blair from the corner of my eye, turning around and tugging at his pants, but he doesn't seem to notice.

Fuck this.

I turn my attention to Percival, who's focused on someone behind me. Parting my lips wide enough, I take him into my mouth, bringing him to the back of my throat, and swallow.

He groans and looks down at me. His smile lifts, and we're immediately in that familiar rhythm. "*Damn.*"

I close my eyes and feel his fingers thread through my hair before I take him out with a *pop*. "Look at *her*."

His smile tilts higher up his tanned cheek. "It's hard with him in my way."

That's when I notice both of his hands behind his head. "Don't stop now, wicked one. Not when the show was just starting."

Smack!

A sharp sting on my ass has me gasping around Percival. Another, and I'm clenching my thighs tight.

"You were always supposed to be *our* toy, Mel."

I hear the stick tumble against the ground the moment Hayse grips my hips and drives into me until his thighs slam against the back of mine, hitting deep enough that I quiver between them.

"Show us you can handle *both* of us." His fingers tighten on my waist as he uses the other to push my head deeper on Percival. He retreats, pulling my head up, only to drive back into me while pushing me down again. Percival groans when he hits the back of my throat.

Wrapping my hair around his fists, Hayse yanks me back to look at him. "That's a start."

Percival laughs. "Climb on, Mi Vera."

I'm being pulled forward by one and pushed by the other. Hayse retreats with a grunt, guiding me onto my husband until I'm fully seated. The pressure against my backside is easier to take than it was the first time, and *so much* better.

I've never been this full. It's… My head fogs with a heated haze. I'm a useless doll between them. The toy they claim I am. And I love it. I'd be whatever they asked me to be right now. The only two men I've ever cared for, who have ever showed an ounce of caring for me.

"Use us, baby."

I move to grip Percival's shoulders, but Hayse holds me back, wrapping his arms around me to keep me tight against him. I can't help but laugh as I use my knees and abs to move, only allowing me short, shallow thrusts.

He's controlling every part of this. Since the moment I walked into this Den, he's been in charge. It's what he's not saying, what his body is doing, that's telling me what I really need to know.

"Mi Vera, are you teasing us?" Percival thrusts into me from below, his hand cupping my breasts before rubbing his thumb over my nipple. Hayse follows that same movement, withdrawing to his tip before driving in with his lips on my neck, twisting and pulling my other nipple between his fingers.

"I can feel him inside you, wicked one." Hayse's sucks on my ear lobe. "I thought *I* was your ruin."

"You are." My stomach clenches. "So, fucking ruin me."

His thrusts grow harder and more deliberate—punishing—his hand wrapping around my throat, whispering heat grazing the back of my ear. "Remember that."

He pushes me forward so I'm flush with Percival, his hands pressing against my back to keep me there. Both of them drive into me at different paces and rhythms. I can feel them growing closer and closer. I reach between my legs, but Hayse pulls it away. "You cum when *I* say."

His fingers press against me, softly circling my clit. He stops just as quickly as he starts because I'm already at the edge.

Smack!

His hand comes hard on my ass again and again with his quickening thrusts. "Let me see you, pretty girl." He brushes the hair that falls to my face, reaches around, and this time when he touches me, I'm clenching around them both.

Percival cups my face, bringing his lips to mine as he spills inside of me. Hayse drags my hips against him until he finds his release.

The moment he does, he's gone. He doesn't stay inside of me or pick me up. He's just gone.

I'm turning to look for him when Raven leans down and pulls Percival's face into hers. His hands fall into her hair, deepening their kiss.

I'm frozen, lost in their kiss. It's so full of passion. It leaves an ache in my chest.

I don't care if Hayse is there, with Blair, or gone; I head to the backroom and shut the door behind me.

Seeing that it's empty, I drop to the mattress, and for the first time in my life, I let myself feel it all. I crumble the wall deep within my chest and allow years of waiting hurt to smother me like it should have long ago.

I hate crying. It's pointless and something I reserve for when I'm in restraints, but I can't stop them. The scalpel to my gut felt better than this. I didn't know what I lost then, but I know Hayse. When my sister disappeared, I didn't let myself feel that loss but it's here now, burning through me right next to losing a mother I never got to know, the brother who abandoned me too young, Percival every time he left, all the times I was left and forgotten in the cells by my father. It's only a matter of time before Raven's gone too.

Everyone leaves. I've known this my entire life so why did I let myself fall this deep?

I don't know how long I'm weeping into the mattress until a soft touch on my forehead startles me awake—barely, I've been through so much the last few days, my eyes are only cracked enough to see his white hair.

"I love you," I say. The timing is horrible, but I can no longer lie.

I feel his lips brush my temple. "I know." My hands are dragged above my head.

"Goodbye, pretty girl."

Darling Devil

My Devil Doll's confession means nothing.

Today is the day I've been waiting for, bidding my time for.

Today is the day she becomes *mine*.

Chapter Sixteen

I'm going to kill him.

Mothering hell.

I tug at the ropes harder. Hayse not only tied me to the bed, but he locked the damn door behind him and has someone playing the piano on a constant to drown out my calls for help.

"Goodbye, pretty girl."

If he thinks this is goodbye, he's out of his mind. It's been hours of working at them, but I'm nearly there. Unlike the shackles in Hayse's room, the ones he tied me with here are made of a softer rope, and although my ring is empty, the edge is sharp enough to slowly slice away at it.

I haven't stopped since remembering Dragon's promise to kill Hayse. No one gets to murder the bastard, except for me.

Snap.

That damn thing in my chest flutters. Using my free hand, I untie the other and both legs before grabbing a silk robe and running out of the Den.

I don't stop. Not when I'm out of the Den's doors, or when I slip on wet dirt, not when I nearly trip into the river, or when I stumble into three people in the palace halls. With everyone at the wedding, I'm not worried about getting caught and dragged back to that torture room.

I rush straight to Hayse's room first. *Empty.* I turn to leave, but the lit hearth catches my eye. His notebooks are up in flames, but it's my melting face that has me looking closer. It's a canvas, a detailed painting of me sleeping and tied to his bed.

"He's at the wedding." I turn, finding Shayla behind me. She's holding a bundle of silk in her arms. "He said if you came, to do everything we could to keep you here. He said that you won't have to worry about anything once it's over. That you'll be safe."

I scoff. "I haven't been safe a day in my life."

She hands me the pile of silk, eyeing the scars on my forehead with a smile. "It's from one of the wise women. She said, knowing you, you'd make a scene at a big event and would need extra protection."

I take the dress in my hands, feeling the thick protective leather beneath it, and smile. "Grim Rose?"

Shayla's toothy grin widens, her fingers fumbling with the belt around her simple chemise, freeing something from the hidden pocket. Grabbing my hand, she unlatches my ring and pinches in a splinter of flax. "I'm no witch, but Kim and Ryan helped bless it. It's another gift for being so kind to us."

"A little love and a splinter of flax is sure to keep your head from the reaper's axe." I bite back my giggle at the childhood rhyme and ominous wave of impending doom that fills the air around us. "It's not the axe witches fear."

Her small arms wrap around my middle, nearly knocking the breath from me. "Please don't die."

I run my fingers over her precious scars. "Impossible, little one."

MALICIOUS INTENTIONS

Walking into a wedding that's presenting Amelvira Aramos and Percival Deimos as a guest was something I was really looking forward to. I planned to be two bottles of red deep in the back of the cathedral with the real Persival and Oliver, maybe sneak some of the cake, start a small fire to panic the aunts. It was supposed to be a fun evening.

Instead, I took out three guards who tried to keep me from coming through, wiping off my bloody hands on their pants.

All heads turn back as the double doors slam behind me.

At least I look good.

The silks weren't a dress as I expected, but a loose, laced top hiding the leather corset beneath. I threw on my leather riding pants, tying them at the sides of my hip. My knee-high boots are paired with the heels that come to sharp points. All cling to my skin like I was made of it.

My hair is styled into horns like the Devil they think I am, and with the stitches gone it looks as if they grew there.

Raven grips my hand, pulling to sit beside her. When I resist and give her a wink, a mischievous smile spreads across her face and she stands at my side, placing her hand on the back of my shoulder to let me know she's with me, that whatever I'm about to do, she has my back.

Looking at the couple on the raised dais, I tilt my head. "Have you objected already?"

Gasps and murmurs rise, but my eyes are locked on Hayse.

Holy hell. With his hands clasped in front of him, the red shirt peaking beneath the otherwise all black attire, he looks... Devilish. The cut on his lip and brow are cleaned up, adding to his brutal beauty.

"You need to leave!" Fern stands, her face as red as her dress, coughing into her hands.

"Oh, but I can't." I take a step forward, cradling my lower stomach. "I'm pregnant. With *his* child!" I point straight to Hayse.

Blair sucks in a startled breath.

Cough. Fern covers her mouth as more erupt from her throat. Heads bob from left to right as a blanket of smoke slithers along the floor, funneling in through the room.

While everyone continues to gasp, roar, and cough, Hayse's head falls back with a bellowing laugh leaving his chest. "You don't disappoint."

"Seize her!" King Hale screams.

Raven pulls me back. "We need to go, Mel. Now!"

I stumble with the force she's tugging on my shoulders.

No. I can't leave. I won't!

I step forward, determined to make my way toward Hayse, but I'm cut off by someone in a black cloak. The dragon mask glistens, looming above me.

"No! You can't kill him!" I knee between his legs, but he catches it before it can strike.

"*Run.*" His voice is stern and harsh, pleading almost.

The arrow in his hand is all I see before he shoves me into Raven, who drags me outside. I yank free from her hold, my fingers fumbling on the door, when I'm lifted off my feet.

"The kings are going to have fun with you."

I can't move my arms with the way the guard is holding me tight against him, but my legs flail as much as they can to throw him off balance. I spot Raven being carried off in a different direction by a royal guard, his fist striking her eye before her body falls limp.

"Rav—"

My ears ring, loud and piercing from the explosion. I crawl to my knees, bracing myself to climb to my feet but can't balance myself enough to stand straight.

Rubble is everywhere with rocks falling from the sky and smoke billowing toward it. The building where the wedding was held is now flattened and screams pierce the ringing pounding against my skull.

Raven… Hayse…

No, no, no!

Without the use of my legs, I crawl, clawing at the grass beneath me to take me closer to the mess.

Black boots cut off my path. I drag my eyes from them to the dreadful Dragon mask hovering over me. "Did you kill him?"

His head tilts with that assessing gaze.

"You killed them!" Fern's sharp wails pull me away. "You animal!"

Dragon turns, his hands wrapping around her neck, shoving her against a tree.

He doesn't see Florence, who rushes me so fast, she's able to kick my jaw hard enough to drop me on my back. "We know you killed our sister."

She's upside down, but I can see the look of horror wash over her as her sister thumps lifelessly to the ground.

She gets one swipe at Dragon, knocking his mask clean off.

My head is spinning. It feels like someone clenched their fists around my lungs and squeezed.

"Hayse?" *But…* I saw Hayse a second before Dragon cut off my line of sight in the cathedral. He can't be Dragon.

Florence sprints away with him hot on her heels.

"Wait!" I stumble onto my feet and follow before they can get too far ahead.

My mouth is dry, filled with debris, and I'm so dizzy that I swear I hear them running behind me, not in front of me. I turn back in case I got mixed up, and sure enough, Dragon is right behind me.

Wait… Didn't he lose his mask?

With my lack of stability, my heels sink into the grass as I make my way toward him. "Hayse, why are you Dragon? How?"

He catches me before I fall but not before I swipe the mask away.

"Percival?" What the fuck is going on?

"Stay here, Mi Vera. I need to find Raven."

"But—" He cuts me a glare that shuts me up.

"I'll be right back." He runs off, disappearing back through the trees.

Snap.

My head twists. "Hayse?"

My heels catch on a twig, sending me straight onto my palms before my body crashes with the ground.

My scalp screams as my head is pulled back by my hair, my body being dragged with it. "Wait! Stop!"

I reach back to grab their hand, needing to relieve the sharp sting, but I only find air. My body is weightless as I watch the cliff rise above me.

I'm falling.

Chapter Seventeen

Now

Every memory strikes so hard, I grip my head to make them stop. Parts of them aren't clear, and every new question I have grows more urgent than the last.

Leaving Raven on the couch, I rush to the washroom and turn to see myself in the mirror, lifting Hayse's tunic to my neck.

A black dragon is inked down the side of my back.

It's breathtaking. There's so much detail, the scales, the claws, the eyes, all of it is a work of art I want to take in, but I'm on the verge of panicking.

If that memory was real, then the others were too.

Without looking at anyone or muttering a single word, I cross the front room and walk out the door. I don't know where I'm headed, just that I need a moment alone, a minute to think, to breathe, to make sense of it all.

The steps that follow me are as familiar as my own. "Which one of you is Dragon? Really?"

Hayse doesn't hide his growing smirk. "You remember?"

"I remember you telling me to kill you. Or was that Percival?"

"Percival only wore the mask in the Den, at the wedding, and again the other day." There's levity in his voice, like it's funny that he sent me on a Trove mission to look into himself.

"Hayse, that's not funny!" I smack his chest before wrapping my arms around his middle, squeezing tighter just because I can, because he's here, *alive.* "I could have killed you. I *wanted* to kill you when I saw you standing at that altar. How——" I stop myself. I'm stuck between needing answers about the Dragon and what happened at that wedding.

He takes my hands, pulling them into his chest to cage me against him. His eyes search mine. "I've hated you my entire life." Not a great start. "I cursed you any chance I could because the secrets you pulled from Percival when you were younger is what led our fathers to use and abuse us. Eventually, I started working with the Trove and learned you were Death's sister. Duke mentioned wanting to bring you on, and I encouraged it because I saw an opportunity. He owed me a favor for helping save his life, so he let me drag you into a fake task I set up. He thinks you're here to look into my father, which isn't entirely untrue since you're looking into me and the overseas bullshit. But it was all a setup to get you to come back to me, so I could use, break, and humiliate you. Only you never broke, and I don't even think you feel things like humiliation."

He pauses to let me catch up to the fact that the last month of my life has been a complete lie.

"You were supposed to be both mine and Percival's. We hated being used, but we also hated being shackled to lives and wives we didn't choose. While he held the same resentment, he had his issues worked out on you over the years, so he agreed to help me with mine."

My stomach sours. It's not his admissions, it's the fact that I caused him and Percival so much pain. He doesn't need to explain it any further because I know. I overheard the kings in that tower. Piecing it all together now, I understand the weight of what I've done.

I deserve whatever he had planned for me.

"What about the explosions?"

"I used the dream draught you supplied me, *Dragon*, with to make the bombs. Percival was supposed to storm in wearing the Dragon mask, and it was going to look like he killed me before the bombs went off and everyone went to sleep. Then I was going to kill the kings myself." He shakes his head. "That was the extent of the plan as of an hour ago, when I realized I couldn't live or die without you. I know it's selfish, but I couldn't stand the idea of you with Percival either. I didn't care if you forgave me for last night or anything else. I was going to come back and take you somewhere no one would find us. But someone switched my draught with real bombs, and with all the chaos, I didn't get a chance to kill any of the kings."

"What was the plan before? Make me hate you enough to *actually* kill you?"

"I deserved it." His lips press against my knuckles. "I've had over a week to consider everything, and the only person I can think of who wasn't there was your father."

I'm not surprised. I should be, but that man hasn't truly surprised me in years. He's capable of anything, and it wouldn't be the first time he bombed a place his own daughter was at.

"How did you find me?" The last thing I do remember is falling over a cliff.

"I heard your screams." He kisses my wrist where a brutal scar is still fresh. "I jumped, knowing I might die if that's where it took me to get to you. There's no amount of suffering I wouldn't endure to be with you, Mel."

My mouth is wide open at the thought of Hayse willingly jumping off a cliff to help me.

"I found what you were looking for." A soft voice has both our heads turning. Dove, dressed as one of the wise women, nudges another cloaked figure forward.

Their hood falls back.

Hayse drops my arms but doesn't let go, taking a step toward her. "Mom?"

Chapter Eighteen

No one talks.

Queen Leila, Hayse's mother, who is supposed to be dead, sits on the chair before us, her back straight as a pin, like any good queen.

Hayse is sitting at my side, his arms crossed over his chest defensively, brows drawn in with confusion as he leans back against the couch.

Except for their black eyes, they look nothing alike. With her long brown hair and King Sterling's black hair, I don't know how Hayse ended up with white. I can sense a familiarity about her, though.

After Blair ensured the fire was roaring and we all had steaming cups of coffee, Queen Leila dismissed her, Percival, and Raven to speak with her son alone. She dismissed me too, but Hayse wouldn't hear it, pulling me beside him with a silent order.

"So, you're not dead."

Queen Leila's eyes drag from her sons to mine with visible struggle to look kind. "You're quite the observer."

"I'm quite a lot of things, but I like to think observing is my best quality." I lean back and kick my leg over my knee to appear relaxed, even though I'm anything but. "Why don't you start from the beginning?"

Dove didn't say goodbye after dropping this bomb in our laps, just, *"Double the price, Mel. When I call for you, you answer."*

As much as I wanted to know about the woman before us, I'm not sure it's worth being indebted to someone like Dove. No one knows what she really looks like, her age, or even her name.

"Well, as you know, our lives as false royalty are to mirror the royals exactly as possible. When Queen Deimos passed, I thought I was going to die as well. *Unfortunately*, that wasn't the case. In the dead of night, I was taken from my bed and shoved onto a boat. I learned then that the unwanted are sold overseas, both false and real royalty. I spent years in torment until I met someone who helped me out of it. They were part of a rogue group called The Strays."

Hayse and I exchange curious glances. The Strays are another silent, vigilante group known to the Trove.

"Don't worry about me, darling, I survived."

A bitter laugh leaves my chest, bringing both of their full attention to me. "You're good, I'll give you that." I twirl my foot. "Even if your story were true, *Raelya*." I watch her face crumble as I say her birth name. The one I know from an old journal my mother left behind. It's not a secret but I want her to know that I'm aware of their past, that I am my mother's daughter and don't take well to liars. It took seeing her to release that old memory. "You knew the kings sold people, which means you were likely aware of the auction, and with your overseas connection, you know about Hayse and Percival's treatment. And yet *you* survived? You're here now, which means you had the means to come here before, and yet you left your son to his own brutal torment."

"That's a stretch." Queen Leila crosses her arms as if I offended her. It's in this exact moment that I see why Hayse hates the gesture.

"Is it?" I turn to speak to Hayse, not wanting to give this woman another second of my time. "Her eyes are heavy, she's yawned twice, and there is a tinge of pink in her hair where she attempted to clean away blood. She was at the wedding."

We're all still feeling the aftereffects of what little draught wasn't replaced by bombs.

"I came for my son!" The queen's eyes sear into mine. "Is that so bad? You think I'm a horrible person? What about you?"

"I do enjoy ruining a perfectly good day for someone else, but it's because of people like you. I would never sell my family."

"That's rich coming from an Aramos——" I stop her with a wave of my hand. A good queen wouldn't have let me.

"You're using someone else's story to make yours plausible." Jax told me his theories about what he believes happened to his little sprite. This is nearly word for word the rumors he's heard mixed with his own beliefs, down to The Strays. "You left on purpose."

Queen Leila's jaw ticks as she jumps to her feet. "I don't have to stay here and be insulted by a lying witch!"

I rise to mine, steady and calm. Without my heels, I'm smaller than her, but I don't feel it. I do, however, feel woozy. "You're working with your husband to build your own empire. The auction, having people overseas tend to Hayse, it's all some sick initiation, isn't it?" I keep going without letting her answer. The ticks on her face are all I need to confirm I'm right. "You came back because King Sterling planned to kill my father *and* King Deimos at the wedding."

Queen Leila's scowl deepens her pretty face. "You think you're so clever. You have no idea what it's taken to secure our own throne overseas. All the years, the planning, the bribing… That auction! If only you knew the truth of how that started, you wouldn't be looking at *me* like I'm the villain." Her head falls back with maniacal laughter. "It helped me in the end though. Your father and King Deimos were so blinded by the money coming in that they didn't realize we had them by the throat.

And then there's you, fucking anyone you were told to, pulling secrets, doing the dirty work we were able to intercept with our spies. Building our own throne was easy, but it was manipulating the kingdoms over here that took work."

"I doubt it." I yawn.

"Really?" she scoffs. "The Whiteharts were easily blackmailed because of King Tydas' harlots. King Aramos is easily blackmailed and a disgrace because one daughter is a whore, his only male heir married a harlot, and the other daughter is completely mental. And then there is King Deimos. Percival is so loyal to Hayse that when his father falls, he won't object to seeing his best friend on a throne. With his marriage to you, once King Aramos falls, we'll have both kingdoms in our pocket. Once the Deimos' didn't have an heir to pass their throne to—"

Hayse leans forward, his elbows resting on his knees. "How the fuck do you know Percival wouldn't have an heir?"

My throat tightens. I can hear her voice so clearly now, I can see the side of her face from where I was strapped to that bed. "It was you." My stomach knots into a thousand tiny braids. "You were the one who ordered the doctor to take it all."

"Like you'd be a good—"

Hayse jumps to his feet, grabs the knife off the counter, and pushes his mother flat against the chair. Her feet kick as she screams with him hovering over her. His back muscles work with the quick back-and-forth motion of his arm.

When he turns, he's splattered in blood, tossing something pink and bloody into the fireplace—her tongue. He cut out her tongue. "Get the ropes from the room."

I cross the small home and find the ropes under the bed. When I return, I see Queen Leila gripping her mouth with blood pouring between her fingers.

Hayse takes the ropes from my hand, focused on securing her to the seat, tying her hands and feet so she can't move or so much as wiggle.

The door burst open.

Blair's eyes are wide on the queen, but it's *her* who Hayse and I are taking in. Her hair, her skin, and her dress are caked in blood.

"What happened?" She cups the queen's face, turning to us with question in her eyes.

"She was going to kill us," I blurt out. The poor thing wouldn't understand anything if it weren't a dire situation.

Her frown deepens. "No. No!" Her back straightens, her hand flinging back before striking the queen across the face. "You said you wouldn't kill her!"

The wave of confusion intensifies when my attention falls on the bubbles floating from the hearth. The fire has stilled entirely while the colorful bubbles float to the ceiling that has turned into a bright rainbow. Blair crosses to the kitchen, grabbing a bouquet of flowers as the ceiling changes to thundering skies.

"Fuck." Hayse grabs my hand. "Ride it out. It's a poison I use to mess with the kings every now and again. It's in the fire."

"You said we can keep her! You promised!" Blair swipes the bouquet of flowers through Queen Leila's stomach that begins spilling glitter.

Hayse moves quick, storming after Blair, but she's faster, grabbing one of the rainbows and… My heart leaps out of my chest as I move.

I know the motions of knocking an arrow.

Chapter Nineteen

This is my nightmare. I've watched everyone I've ever loved leave me, but Hayse…

There is no stopping the arrow from penetrating straight through his chest. All I can do is catch his head before it hits the table. Even with my hand to break most of the impact, it's hard enough that his eyes roll to the back of his head.

No! No, no, no. "Hayse," I tap his cheek. "Wake up. You don't get to leave me."

He doesn't stir after one tap, not two, not three…

"Why?" I toss my head over my shoulder and see the door is open just enough to show Percival lying unconscious on the ground outside the cabin. Raven is gagged and tied by her own dress next to the stump with the axe. Tears fill her eyes, her head shaking side to side, taking in Percival's still form.

"*They* weren't going to let me have you!" Her eyes soften as if that's a reasonable explanation. "But Queen Leila and King Soren said that after the wedding, I'd get to keep you all to myself. Then I heard them talking about your escape from the tower. King Soren said he wanted you for himself!" Her chest rises and falls rapidly as she closes in. "I couldn't let that happen. Hayse was one thing. He was my connection to you. We could both have him, but no one else was to be with you!"

"Did you poison Raven? Set off the bombs in the cathedral?" Raven swore up and down that she never stole the powder in my ring, and I believe her. Not only did she not hold any signs of lying, but I trust her with my life.

Blair falls to her knees, cupping my cheeks with her delicate hands. It takes every ounce of me to stay still and not flinch from her. When I see her eyes, I don't want to. Whatever drug she put in that fire is hypnotizing me in her true eyes, not the purple contacts, but the spinning greens.

"I saw you tied up in Hayse's bed and took your powder. You're so much better when you're your most raw, authentic self, and you don't need Raven because you have me. I'm more like you than she is. I *am* you, Mel." She tucks a lock of hair behind my ear. "When I first saw you with Percival, you were so pretty, so perfect. I only went to the balls because I knew you would be there. I followed Hayse and Percival around for any crumbs of information on you. That's how I knew to follow Hayse and learned all about the Trove and his task for you. When he said you looked like the Devil's doll, that's what I became for you. Your own personal Darling Devil. I realized that you would never accept me the way I am. You needed someone to taunt you, to be just as twisted and malevolent as you are.

"Don't you see that no one else cares for you? I only had to make a passing comment to Oliver that you've been leading him on, and he was ready to take what he thought he was owed. And your father just needed to overhear me talking about Hayse's popularity with the overseas kingdoms to send you to that pirate. Your brother hates you. Your sister doesn't notice you. Percival prefers other women. Hayse… I thought telling the kings about you and Hayse would finally put an end to it, and it did in a way. He tried to end it with you. I would never—"

She pulls me in, pressing her lips against mine, wrapping her hands behind my head. When she backs away, her eyes lock on where her fingers trail through my hair that looks like thin slithering snakes.

"You told me to take what I wanted without apologizing for it, and I'm not going to." Her lips press harder, her tongue nudging my mouth open. "We can stay here forever."

I crawl back on my hands, coaxing her mouth farther into mine to follow. My only focus is getting her as far away from Hayse as possible. I'm still deep in this high, so I'm only slightly positive the flower in her hand is a knife.

My groan catches between us when my back hits something hard. I don't need long. I've used my body for worse things than saving my life.

Wrapping my hand into her locks, I deepen the kiss, my tongue wrapping around hers.

Her fingers trail up my thighs. "I'm so happy you survived that fall. I didn't mean to toss you off. I tried to help you up, but I tripped. I thought… I thought you were dead. I thought it was over."

Snap!

"It is for *you*." Raven plunges the broken spindle into Blair's neck.

Pain slices me open. The rose Blair had was a knife after all.

As she falls over, the blade slides out of me, blood spilling like fine wine from a cracked barrel. The world around me fades into reality. There are no rainbows, bubbles, or flowers. There is, however, a lot of warm, sticky blood pooling into my lap.

If I'm dying, it's not going to be alone on the damn floor. I toss Blair off me and scoot toward Hayse. Raven curses, putting pressure on my stomach as I grip his hand.

Sucking in a sharp breath, I look over my ring that scratches at my finger. Something white pokes out of it.

The moment I unlatch the secret cavity a small amethyst ring tumbles to my chest. The tiny, folded piece of paper that was hidden within it has perfect penmanship:

My entire life has been hell because of you, Amelvira Lunasol Aramos. That name alone has caused me so much misery and pain, but it also gave me purpose. I knew when I set out to ruin your life that I would end mine, but it wasn't supposed to end yours. I didn't expect you, Mel. I didn't expect to find what I've always wanted, the thing I didn't believe I deserved. You're not my other half, but my equal in every sense. Your wickedness and chaos sings to mine, and I'll never live another day without you in it, beside me.

As I write this, you're sleeping, muttering filthy things about me, and it's taking all my self-control not to slap you awake so I can do them. But I need you to wake up so I can give you this ring. Because with you, I never want the days to end, the dreams, the nightmares. I want it all with you.

Gripping the letter, I tell Raven, "Find Jax."

"It had to be the gut, Princess?" Jax's hands are caked in blood as he works the needle through my stomach.

I attempt a smile, but it comes out with a scream from the slicing pain.

"Make her scream one more time." Hayse threatens him by tossing a knife in the air and catching it. His head and shoulder are bleeding, but he ignored all my pleas to patch himself up first so he could work on my stomach before Jax arrived. He knows little about healing, but he said he's worked with Silas a few times to not only save Duke's life but also Cain and Dove's during a brutal attack with a priest.

By the time Raven returned with Jax, I only needed stitches. While he started on me, she focused on waking and patching up Percival, who was hit over the head with a rock by Blair.

"I hate myself," she mutters while grabbing water from the kitchen. "I should have seen what she was. When I worked for Silas, that's what I did. I saw people for who they really were."

"By fucking them." Percival takes the water she offers after wrapping her head and shoulder where Blair attacked her. "You weren't fucking her so don't blame yourself. We grew up with her, we should have seen who she was throughout the years."

He doesn't let her frown for a second before he's wrapping his arms around her. The kiss on her forehead warms my heart.

I bite a sharp groan when the needle hits me again. "You weren't this bad with the forehead."

Hayse's head swings back toward Jax. "*You* did that to her?"

He holds his hands up in self-defense, the string attached to me pulling with the needle he's holding. "Shit, sorry." He lowers his hands. "She asked me to. We have a strict agreement that doesn't allow me to deny her such requests."

I take his nipple between my fingers, twist, and pull. "Shut the hell up before he actually kills you."

"She said she wanted to make a little girl smile," he tells Hayse. "I have a soft spot for such a thing."

Hayse grunts, but he doesn't stab him or cut out his tongue, so it must be a good sign.

When Jax is done, Hayse walks to Blair's body, where she's lying in front of the roaring hearth. "It's time to see if witches burn." With the point of his boot, he kicks her in next to his burning mother.

"I'm not even going to ask why we just murdered the princess." Jax swipes the wine off the table, finishes half before handing the rest to me. My pain tolerance is higher than most, but I don't hesitate to take the edge off.

When Hayse turns back, I see all the questions, all the scenarios that have played through my head running through his. He spots the amethyst on my finger and grins.

MALICIOUS INTENTIONS

I always thought I needed to belong somewhere, to become what people said I was—the evil, wicked, Satan Spawn with the cursed eyes who wreaks havoc wherever I go, to do whatever my father needed me to at the expense of my body, ingesting powders to dull myself, striving to be part of the Trove.

With Hayse, I don't need any of it. I don't need to put on a show or drown myself with wine or distractions.

I'm just me.

Swooping me gently into his arms, Hayse steps out the door, kissing my temple under the night sky. "Pick your kingdom, pretty girl."

Epilogue
Mel

"You love her?" The question fills me with a rush of emotions, a conflicting mix of warm elation and grief. Everything is crashing down at once, the aftereffects of the inhaled drugs making any semblance of sadness into a hurricane of tears, mild annoyance into a storming rage, and glimpse of happiness into a rush of overbearing joy.

Blair tried to fuck and kill me, my father has been selling me for years, the kings bought me to use and torture me, Hayse's mother was never dead but played a role in selling him, and the task I was given had been a ruse set by my husband and his best friend, who I fell in love with.

Percival's laugh is light, his cheekbones angled with genuine mirth, shadowed under the night sky. "Raven is… If love means you'd do anything to save them then yes, with all my heart."

My brow rises but before I can pry any more from him, a figure breaks the tree line surrounding our cabin. He's so fast that I don't have time to do anything but freeze as his arms wrap around my shoulders.

"I'm only saying this once so enjoy it while it lasts." Cain doesn't pull away as his words meet my ear. "I'm so sorry that I was too stubborn and lost in my own shit that I blamed and hated you, but I'm even more sorry that I wasn't there for you."

"Cain—"

"You're nothing like him. I shouldn't have said you were." He pulls back, his dark eyes glossy. "You don't deserve any of the shit you've been through and it's my fault for not listening, for running away when you and Eva needed me most."

Spotting Percival and Duke watching us, his words surround me like a warm cloak on a hot summer day. My brother isn't one to apologize, and certainly not with others around to hear it.

"You're causing a scene." I give him my best smirk as a tear slides down my cheek. "That's my thing."

He lifts my hand with his, the amethyst ring shining between us, breaking the uncomfortable tension of feeling neither of us likes to drown in. "You'll get your chance at another soon enough."

The cabin door opens and closes with an audible lock clicking into place. All of our heads twist to find Hayse, Raven, and Jax emerging from the cabin.

"You'll always be Mi Vera," Percival whispers as he passes me to meet Raven, draping his arm around her shoulder.

"Ready?" Hayse laces his fingers through mine.

"I've never been *ready* for anything," I rise to my toes and kiss him softly. "And I'm not about to start preparing now." Because as long as I'm with him, I don't care what happens next.

Hayse

Three Months Later

Mel's jaw drops when she walks through the glass conservatory, the full moon high and bright above the vast dome. Candles adorn every inch of this place, carefully placed away from the lush greenery and flowers to avoid any accidental fires.

There aren't any gold or ornamental decorations out here, just everything and everyone she loves in one place.

She had no part in this. The woman not only can't cook but getting her to plan anything is next to impossible.

Everyone tried to help, Raven, Eva, Audrey, Shayla, Mel's twin nieces, but I wouldn't let them. They all know pieces of her, but this isn't about them and the parts they know. It's *my* gift to her.

Percival shows me up by rubbing his eyes when he sees her walking down that aisle.

The last time I saw her walk down an aisle, I already knew I would marry her. She came barreling in, horns on her head, heels announcing her entrance. The second she screamed to the world that she was pregnant with my child only solidified that I would murder her father for taking that chance away from us.

I have never once been truly envious of Percival but hearing that she was pregnant with his child made me want to burn him at the stake. Every part of me then shattered for him, hearing it was taken too soon.

With the vows I'm about to make to her, I'm adding one to myself: I will murder her father for what he's done to her. For all of it.

This day isn't about him, though.

As Mel continues down the aisle, taking in every inch of the lush conservatory, I take her in. Everything is black. Her heels, the off the shoulder dress that slits up her legs, the lace veil trailing behind her. Her hair shines brighter, a silver hue under the moon.

With the scars on her head, she looks every bit of the temptress she is.

"Why is he crying?" She nods toward Percival standing behind me.

"He loves happy endings," Raven whispers behind her.

A royal wedding should be massive, elaborate, filled with people who hand over gifts, but we didn't want any of that. Cain sits with his wife Audrey and their daughters, Delany and Alison. Mel's twin, Eva, is with her husband, Silas. Jax is looking at Mel with a strange longing that's about to put him back on his ship if I'm nice. And then there are the three children, Shayla, Kim, and Ryan.

Mel said if she couldn't adopt Raven, she would settle for them. They don't have parents. They're orphans my father brought in to be raised by the servants to eventually serve. Not anymore.

The amethyst ring I slide over her finger really was one of the first things I ever made. I just didn't elaborate as to why I made it.

Unlike many of the other princes, I did want to marry one day. Having a father who abused me and a mother who abandoned me, had me striving for what I didn't have. Hookups were empty and meaningless with people who couldn't handle the full brunt of what I craved. When I finished the ring, I swore I'd find someone to give it to, someone who was real, who wouldn't break, who wouldn't run, who matched me in every way.

Mel came in and burned the mundane into a disastrous masterpiece. Chaos and beauty all wrapped in a blonde, black bow.

After finding her at the bottom of the cavern, wrapped in a tomb of thorns, I wasn't going to waste another second not worshiping her if she woke up. I prayed to every divinity I could think of for help.

And when she finally did and her memories were gone, I saw the perfect opportunity to fuck with her a little longer. I can't help it. She's so cute when she's angry, and there's something about her potentially killing me that jump-starts my heart.

Mel slides a thick black ring onto my finger. "This is a bit fancy for me, no?"

She laughs. "You gave me yours, it's only fair I give you mine."

It's all over too quick. Just like Percival and Raven's was last week.

Since only King Aramos, Deimos, and Soren knew about the marriage between Percival and Mel, it was easy to burn the evidence. The problem was between Mel and me. Our marriage was still technically illegal, but she renounced her role as an Aramos heir.

In doing so, she became a queen. *My* queen.

"They've been holding on longer than I thought." Cain pulls the knife from my father's shoulder, his shrieks echoing through the wide-open air.

Duke shakes his head from the corner. The man never enjoys the fun. Not unless his life is on the line.

"Might I suggest cutting off their hands?" Jax holds up a meat cleaver and a bottle of rum.

"That's going to be harder to heal, but I do need the practice for whenever Duke inevitably loses an appendage," Silas says while stitching up King Deimos' ribs.

Mel noticed a scar on mine where my father had taken the cane too hard on me years ago and came here to give him a deeper one. "I can fix those scars so they're thinner and less noticeable." Silas nods toward her forehead.

"No need. You don't need to stitch him up either." I can see the tension she feels being in this room, but also the relief that we no longer need these two.

Cain had told us that his father kindly suggested he and Audrey leave before things got out of hand at my wedding to Blair, to which Cain sent Audrey off, instructing her to tell Duke to come immediately. He and Cain overheard the idiots talking about finding Mel to imprison her for good. Little did they know Cain no longer despises his sister.

They've been useful in testing new weapons I've been working on for the Trove. I usually have to bide my time and kidnap one of the people I'm forced to fuck.

Taking the meat cleaver from Jax, I don't let either of them enjoy another breath before I'm bringing it to their necks. It's messy, with blood spraying in every direction, but the second I know they won't be able to hurt us again a weight lifts off my shoulders.

They may be our fathers, but they were our tormentors first. Blood means nothing. I feel nothing but freedom killing them. Guilt and regret prickle at me for not doing it sooner.

We allowed them to live this long to gather as much information as we could about the auction. Jax got what he needed to find whoever it was he was searching for.

When I turn and see my wife's violet eyes, the heated hunger behind them, I order everyone out.

Duke smirks for the first time tonight. "I'm late for a date with my little monster anyway."

Cain slams his fist into Duke's side with a taunting laugh just before the door closes.

I don't know what it is about watching me hurt people who have caused her any sort of harm, but it turns Mel into an absolute menace.

The weapon is still sticky in my hands when she jumps on me, wrapping her legs around my torso. My back hits the table holding the lifeless kings. She reached between us and pulls me free, stroking me quickly before easing herself on.

I toss the cleaver to the side to grip her better, walking us to the wall so I can lift the chains to her wrists. Pulling the excess ends, her arms fling out to the sides.

Still inside her, I press her back against the wall and pull out just enough to drive my full length back in. It doesn't matter that she can't finish with penetration, she moans and screams my name for more. I'm not giving up, though. It only means that I get to touch her, taste her, and fuck her longer trying.

When I toss the shirt over my head, her grin lifts even higher, her eyes latching onto the dragon peeking over my shoulder. After finishing hers, I made her tattoo me right back.

"You want a better view?"

I drop to my knees, toss her leg over my shoulder, and devour every inch of her, worshipping *my wife* with praises meant just for her. "I love you, pretty girl."

I'll kill for you, die for you, but I vow to live long enough to watch you burn this world to ashes. I have the matches in my pocket.

Epilogue

Hayse

Sixteen Years Ago

My father is hosting the kings in his chambers, which means Percival is somewhere around here. Even though he lives in his manor up the hill, he's here more than his home. At first, I thought it was because he had a crush on Blair or the other princesses who never want to leave when he's around, but when he comes, he drags me through the woods in search of some mysterious Den that supposedly houses naked women.

I've heard of it, *the Forbidden Den*, but I don't care about watching women dance around. I rather run or draw, do something useful.

I follow the hall to his chamber, which is next to mine, when I spot him. He's smirking at a girl with light hair who's holding her hands behind her back in the way Blair does when she wants me to notice her. Something her aunts told her to do to all the princes.

Neither of them notices me walking toward them, and that sours something deep in my stomach. They only have eyes for each other.

When I see her eyes, it's as if the world stops. She still hasn't seen me, but I see *her*. Those eyes. It's like the sun shining on sparkling amethysts, and the stone kept a ray for itself. My feet fumble under me, but they're already behind his closed door by the time I work up the nerve to call for them.

I rush to my chambers, cross the room, pass my bed, and head straight for my wardrobe that attaches to his. Pushing aside the hidden compartment, I'm about to jump out and scare them when I'm caught by the sight of her again.

I frown. Her laugh is all wrong. It's not real. It's too high and she does that thing where she touches his leg repetitively. He notices it too, but not in the same way I do. His cheeks pink, and he looks at her like she's a holy deity.

"You should mind your tongue." He laughs with her. "If someone heard you say such wicked things—"

"Would that I could." This time, she grazes his arm. "Come on, Perce, you must know something fun about this place."

Perce?

"Well…" His fingers tangle with hers. "My father is building a menagerie for King Soren, with all the exotic animals they've been dealing with overseas. And we do have those *sex* dens." He whispers the last part.

She gasps. "Why would you need dens for that?"

I can see what she's doing, and I don't blame him for telling her our kingdom's most prized secrets. If she had asked me, I would have told her anything she wanted to hear.

And I hate her for it. I hate that she chose him to go to when this is *my* home. It's probably my white hair or the birthmark. All the other royals mock me for it, saying I look too weird to be a real royal, so they made me a false one.

Percival shrugs.

I watch them for an hour before King Aramos collects her for a few minutes before returning her. When she comes back this time, her face is brighter than ever.

It's another hour before King Aramos returns to collect them both. I follow, too intrigued as to why I wasn't called on.

When the door to my father's chambers shuts, I lean my ear against it, hearing them faintly but enough to comprehend.

"Neither of you will court. Do you understand?" King Deimos asks angrily.

"Why not?" Percival whines.

Smack!

"From this day forward, Amelvira Lunasol Aramos is your wife. But no one else must know. Hayse will wed Blair Somberlain when we decide the time is right."

My stomach drops. I don't want to wed Blair. She's so boring.

It feels like a splinter got stuck in my chest. How do I hate someone I've never spoken to, and also angry that she's someone I could never have?

Rustling comes from behind the door. I rush to hide behind the corner, so they don't see me spying. There's obvious tension as King Aramos and Amelvira say their goodbyes and walk off.

"You've never made me prouder than you have today. You got exactly what we needed to form that alliance."

As they pass, I can see her eyes sparkle at his praise. She's the prettiest girl I've ever seen.

I hate her.

Mel wasn't born wicked.

Keep reading for a *Before the Horns* bonus chapter.

Before the Horns

Sixteen Years Ago

Age Eight

Everywhere I search for Eva she's nowhere to be found. I swear that girl can get lost right in front of me. Her nose is always one of those books that she won't stop yapping about, full of princesses and princes.

Hello? We are princesses, why would she need to read about them? Those aren't real stories. True love doesn't exist, although she swears she'll find it one day to prove me wrong.

I hope she does.

I much prefer her books about the witches who eat children. Now *that* is a story I can get behind.

I double back to the kitchens and library without any luck. There's one place I haven't looked. The one place we aren't allowed.

Eva's not one to break the rules; that's much more a me or Cain thing.

The soles of my feet surge with a deep pain *still* after two weeks of healing the burns from those stupid shoes. We should have been more careful talking to those boys in town. Father overheard Eva telling me she thought one was cute, and it earned us an hour of dancing in heels he personally picked and filled with coal.

If my feet hurt this bad, then Eva probably thought to search for the soothing salve down here too.

The basement isn't locked as usual, which only furthers my suspicions.

"Eva?" I call, closing my eyes as I descend the stairs. I've always hated heights. It doesn't matter how high I am, I've gotten dizzy when I roll to the edge of my bed and look down.

Nausea fills my stomach and my head spins as I begin my descend. I call for my twin again.

Nothing.

When I reach the bottom, the sconces aren't well lit, leaving the dark hallway mostly shadows. Our father kept us in these dungeons when we were younger to ensure we were never scared of the dark, but right now, I can't ignore the hairs rising on the back of my neck.

"Eva?" I whisper this time. I don't believe in ghosts or demons, but if they did exist, it would be down here, where the shadows can cloak them.

I'm ready to turn back when I hear faint murmurs. I follow it down the rows of cells, the iron bars, and closets, until I reach the door the soft whines come from.

Sliding the feeding hole to the side, I peer in. A girl is chained to a bed, her arms are tied behind her back, with a bag over her head. The murmurs are coming from her throat. It sounds as if she's trying to scream but can't.

I step back until my back hits the wall.

This can't be real. Why would a woman be tied up down here?

I run back upstairs as fast as I can, slamming right into Mrs. Platewell's pudgy middle. "Amelvira! Tell me you were *not* in the basement!"

"I—" I can't lie. If that girl needs help, I have to tell her. "There's a girl in the basement. She—"

Her hand slams against my mouth. "Enough of your twisted lies. Never speak of this again and never go back down there." She bends to my level, shaking my shoulders. "Do you understand me?"

By the time I return to my room, I find Eva, her legs crossed at the ankles lying on my bed. Jumping next to her, I tell her everything.

Of course, she doesn't believe me. I don't know why. I don't lie. I hate it. It's pointless and makes people look dumb when they're caught in one.

I'm ready to beg her to believe me, to drag her down there so she can see I'm not lying, when the door bursts open. My father walks in, tells Eva to find Mrs. Platewell and help her with dinner while he has a word with me.

Those hairs on the back of my neck perk back up.

When the door closes, my father turns to me. "If you think you're so clever at unraveling secrets, I have something you might be of use for."

That's not as bad as I thought. Better than hot coals or being thrown into a tub of toads and snakes.

I was wrong.

Part of me was wrong. I've never felt as elated as when my father told me he was proud of me for getting the information he needed to secure the Deimos alliance, although I didn't think I'd come home a married girl at the age of eight.

Cain will know what to do. He always makes Eva and me feel better after Father's outbursts or brutal trainings.

"Where are you going?" My brother is headed out the door with our footman.

His head falls the way it does when he's annoyed, his black hair shaking as he turns toward me. That's one thing everyone in this family has in common, black, sable hair. Except for me; I inherited my mother's silver-blonde.

"You're as wicked as they say. I never believed it until…" He spits at my feet. "You're *dead* to me."

My heart shatters in my chest. All the praise my father bestowed on me is now gone, out the door to wherever Cain went. Eva's my twin, my other half, but Cain… Cain has been my light. Eva has her books, but I have—I *had*—him.

I guess I'll have Percival soon enough. He seemed nice.

Feelings aren't for me. I don't like feeling them, which is why I head to my room and hide myself in my washroom, pulling out the mortar and pestle and all the other herbs and flowers I've been drying. From what I've gathered through little questions I've asked Mrs. Platewell, and my mother's diary that I found in the library, witchcraft is precise. It's about the right ingredient and intention.

And, like my mother, my intention is to make something that will help me not feel the pain slicing through my chest.

Fifteen Years Ago

Age Nine

Cain is back today.

It's been a year without letters. A year without a single word about how he's doing in the military. A year of trying not to think about how we left things.

"I need a favor." Those are his first words as he walks through the door.

"Anything."

"Eva wrote about how you made a poison. That you *accidentally* killed the rabbits with it."

"It was an accident!" I had no idea what I made. I had been mixing different things together, jotting them down in journals to figure out what combinations cause specific reactions. There aren't a lot of grimoires lying about, so I'm making my own.

"I need it. No questions asked."

I raise my brow. "Father taught us better than that. I won't ask, but you *will* tell."

He huffs but doesn't walk away. The look of desperation washes over him, and he knows I can tell if he's lying, so he's working out how much of the truth to tell me. "I want to kill the father of a girl I loved."

No ticks on his face. Father taught us all how to lie, but there are always tells and he shows none of them.

"Do you need bait?"

His head jerks. "You're nine. What bait could you be for me?"

Father's been passing me around all the princes to learn secrets that lie within other kingdoms. The most recent was the Whitehearts. Prince Silas is broody but sweet and reminds me a lot of Cain, but it's his brother Holden who really held my attention. There's something inside him that speaks to me, something dark that I couldn't penetrate.

I shrug. Everything about Cain has changed. His back is straighter, his tone is sharper. He's starting to sound more like Father with the hint of authority bitten in his tone.

"Nothing, I guess. But you owe me."

If I find a way in which he does, I'll cash it. I'm just glad that he needs me and there's something still holding us together.

Thirteen Years Ago

Age Eleven

"Aramos' aren't weak!"

Eva and I hardly shiver in the snow at this point. It's been years of him training this weakness out of us.

It's Eva I'm worried about. She tries so hard to be strong, but she's too soft at heart.

We both notice the change in Father's demeanor—the *episode*. Gripping Eva's hand, I stand my ground, but my father takes mine and drags me inside, leaving my sister in her night slip all alone in the dark.

"Rosebud! What are you doing out there? You're going to catch a cold." He drapes a blanket over my shoulders. His back stiffens.

Fuck.

"Daddy, it's me. It's Mel."

"Who were you meeting out there? Was it *him?*"

"No! Daddy, It's Mel! Amelvira!"

"Don't lie to me!" Spit trickles down his lips. He grips my wrists so hard I yelp. My feet feel like they're dragging through honey until he lifts me over his shoulder and walks me down the basement stairs. "I don't know why you make me do this."

My stomach seizes, my eyes shut tight when I see the height I'm at. I don't open them again until my back slams against the tough cot. The door slams shut with a flickering half-tapered candle in the corner casting dimmed, buttery light down the familiar dungeon.

I run and slam my fists against the door. "I'm not mommy! Please! It's me, Amelvira!"

It's been a few days.

The bucket in the corner hasn't lost its pungent smell, yet.

I'm not old enough, but he did put me in the comfy room, where he stores the old wine with the faded rose label. The ones he calls "vintage," meaning they soured before he had a chance to drink them. I don't mind one bit. They help me lose track of time down here, and my spells are rhyming more with every passing day.

I'm pretty sure I rhymed *feather* with *bedridden* and I'm not entirely sure it doesn't work.

The wine is almost gone.

I've resorted between trying to piss in the bottles and transferring the bucket to them.

It's disgusting. I don't recommend anyone stay in a basement for this long without food or water.

I already have the story I'm going to tell Eva. Father sent me away to meet with princes, and I rode a massive steed. I fell off and a prince kissed it all better. She loves that nonsense.

Ten Years Ago

Age Fourteen

Flirting is exhausting.

Exhausting isn't the right word.

Boring.

It's so easy to touch someone's hand or giggle at them, wink, or puff out my chest to get them to spill their secrets. It's both boys and girls that my father has been sending me to. The girls were surprisingly easier than the men, and I'm pretty sure it's because we all just want someone to see us.

I'm an asshole, that's what I am. The problem is, I love it. I love succeeding at something I was supposed to do. The more I get people to tell me their darkest secrets, however small, the more sparkly my insides feel.

That lady who told me I was meant for evil was right. I've been fighting this growing urge to become the horrible names they call me because of the color of my eyes—demonic, hellish, cursed, damned, black-souled.

A rumor starts, and it spreads like wildfire.

It only reminds me of Cain.

Since he's been in the military and refused to write me back, I've been getting updates from Eva—okay, *I'm* Eva. She's always had books, but Cain was mine, so she lets me write him under her name.

I tell him about me from her perspective, and the only positive thing I've received is:

Mel will be fine. Since the Devil made her, she's made of stronger things than we are. I'm sure she's taking everything they say and proving them right anyway. Think about it, Eva. They call her a witch, and she makes poisons. Someone threw a blackberry at her and she ate it, right? Never worry about someone who will take the rock you throw at them and use it as a pillow.

He's not wrong.

I just hate that he's not here. With Eva so in her head all the time, I only have Father.

He is who I'm searching for, determined to find a way to bring Cain back. In his letters, he mentioned an old lover, Audrey, passing away a few years ago. Maybe he's lonely. We can find a princess to introduce him to, or—

I twist the handle of his door and push, ready to give him my best argument, when I still, unable to take another step or so much as take in another breath.

"*King Aramos*," a woman moans with her naked back to me. Her dark brown hair shakes behind her until it hits the sheets wrapped around her waist, where she's bouncing up and down on the bed.

"Damn Leila," my father grunts. "If you keep that up, I'm putting a prince in you."

"Do it!" she yells. "Sterling thought I was dead, and now he thinks I'm still overseas. He won't know."

Smack!

"I have enough heirs! Now are you going to be my Rosebud for the night, or not?"

The woman stills. I need to leave. Every appendage is screaming for me to go, but I'm frozen. I've never been someone to freeze in a situation until this very moment.

It's my father's back to me now.

I can't see this. My feet finally move, taking me through the halls and back toward my room, only I don't want to go there. I can't be in the same home as my father, doing *that* with another woman.

That name, *Rosebud*, is my father's nickname for my mother. I can't understand why tears fall down my cheeks, but they do.

I don't bother with a cloak as I continue running until I'm out the door. There are paths Cain showed me to take where the guards wouldn't spot me if I ever needed to get away. I take these at least twice a year.

They lead me to the river where I swear I saw someone passing by in a cloak, but we live in the middle of nowhere and it's much too dark for someone to be walking through the forest at this time of night.

Then again, here I am in only my night slip, pacing up and down the river's edge.

I stay, thinking of nothing as the cricket chirps turn to singing birds and the twinkling stars brighten with the amber and violet horizon.

By the time I'm back in my room, ready to slumber away the disgusting images, guards barge in to search my room. "Eva?"

"What's going on?" I ask.

"Nothing, Princess."

Nothing isn't nothing at all.

My sister is gone.

Eva vanished four days ago. One of the guards claims to have seen Prince Silas Whitehart's cloak in the woods earlier that day.

King Whitehart and King Deimos are here to discuss that matter, and all my snooping around the door only led me to learn that Prince Silas Whitehart is also missing.

Leave it to Eva to find a prince to disappear with.

"Sneaking around, wife?"

My heart jerks. Prince Percival leans against the wall behind me. He's taller than before. His brown hair, round brown chocolate eyes, and tan skin all sharper and more distinguished than I remember.

"Looking for you, husband." I straighten my dress and thread my arm through his.

"I'm sorry about your sister."

My throat works to swallow the lump in it. I want to believe that Eva disappeared with that prince, but she would have told me if she were seeing someone. She's never mentioned a prince, except the ones in those damn books.

"It's not your fault."

"Most people say *thank you* after a comment like that."

"If you want my thanks, you'd have to do something to earn it, not mumble useless words."

He bites his bottom lip, a smirk threatening to escape its grate. "I do remember when you visited the palace I showed you my chambers. I've been intrigued to learn what secrets my wife holds in hers."

I push the door open with my back. "Behold all the secrets you could ever wish for."

I'm an organized chaos. The paintings on my wall change depending on my mood, the makeup and perfumes on my vanity are there because they provide nothing for my creations. They smell okay, I guess. My bed isn't made, ever. I don't let the maids do it either because it's a waste of everyone's time.

I detest things that are done simply because that is how they are done. I will never be one to make her bed because I will be crawling back into it within a few hours to make the same mess.

Said mess is exactly where Percival leads me, his hand sliding to grip my hand more intimately.

"I'm going to be blunt, so I apologize if it's too much for you to handle." He takes a shaky breath but something about his words irritates me. He thinks I can't *handle* words? "I've had urges, but I don't want to be the kind of husband who steps out on his wife. We're married," his fingers tighten in mine, resting them on his lap, "and husbands and wives—"

"I know," I cut him off. I don't know if I'm ready for this, but I understand what he's saying, or rather, what he's not saying. I can't deny that his fingers feel good in mine. I can't deny that my belly flipped when I looped my arm in his and our hips brushed, or that when he smiled at me my cheeks burned.

I wrap my arms around his neck, reveling in the smile lifting higher on his face.

I don't have a single clue what I'm doing, but I lean in anyway. When our lips touch, it's hard, and my lips pinch between our teeth. He grasps the back of my head, moving me at different angles. I follow his lead, letting him do whatever he needs to.

That urge he mentioned is building in me too when his fingers fall to my back and he pulls the string that holds me tightly together. Our lips remain sealed, finding a steady rhythm until my corset drops to my feet.

I swear he can feel my pulse pounding through every inch of my skin. I hate this… the waiting. His fingers slowly lift the hem of my dress, but I can't take this slow pace anymore.

Pulling away from him, I lift my chemise over my head, watching his eyes fall down my naked body.

He's quick to remove his jacket and top. "Get in the center of the bed."

I climb up and place myself where I think I'm supposed to be while he removes the rest of his clothes. He cups between his legs as he crawls over me. "I've been told this hurts."

"Have you hurt other girls?"

"No!" he answers quickly. "I meant it when I said I want to be loyal to you. It's just that we're taught to be gentle the first time because it can hurt the woman."

"No one told me that." I gulp. I'm not scared of pain. It can't be worse than coal in shoes or watching my brother hate me before my very eyes without an explanation.

He presses my knees apart, settling between them. I've never felt so vulnerable in my entire life. I'm a little worried about the pain now.

His palm roams over my breasts. A spark shocks my entire body when his lips press against one.

"*Oh,*" comes out of my mouth when I feel him against my center. Is that the pain? That's not so... My teeth clench, my eyes sealing tight as a pressure builds in my stomach with a *pop* that makes my eyes water.

Percival's groans are hot against my neck. "Thank you."

I smile up at him. "You're welcome?"

"I'm not finished, I just, I've wanted to know what that felt like for so long."

I can't stop the laugh that leaves me. His matches mine, and we sit here, laughing, connected and understanding each other on a different level than I've ever had with anyone else.

When he's finished, we lie on my bed and talk for hours. His father is horrid, but he has a friend nearby that he runs to. Said friend also has a prick of a father, and he tries to be there for him as much as he can but it's never enough.

He's okay with our marriage, but he does want to be honest about the urges if they come up. I tell him not to worry until we're officially married, meaning when our doubles marry. As of right now, no one knows we're legally married, so what's the harm? We agree to be friends until then, allowing each other to be with anyone, experience anything we wish until the day our doubles walk down that aisle, making us official.

He's not my *one true love,* as Eva would say, but I understand the concept now. Percival is my...

"Mi Vera."

"What?"

"That's what you are to me." He pulls me against him. "I want you by my side for the rest of my life."

It's been six years since I first made this climb and found what I wish I hadn't.

I make the same climb down the stairs to the basement that I do every year, checking for any signs of a woman tied up and locked away.

I know I won't find anything but——

My feet still. A low humming comes from the room that's haunted me for years. I shake my head. It's not real. I'm hearing things. I must be.

As I slide the food slit over, I see what I was hoping wasn't real.

A man is tied to a chair. His back is pouring blood, his head is tucked against his chin.

His shaggy chocolate hair is too familiar.

Prince Silas.

It's been ten months since he and Eva disappeared, which means he's been down here all this time.

Father went on a rampage and fired every single person who worked for us; guards, servants, tailors, seamstresses, and scullions. It was during one of his episodes, and he stopped trusting those around him. Everyone but Mrs. Platewell, her son Splint, and their cousin Blaise. The two newer guards are young, maybe twenty, and by his side at all times. The way they look at me makes my skin crawl and lock my chamber doors before bed.

I can't let Silas disappear like our servants or the woman I found here long ago.

Taking the hanging keys, I unlock the door and grab a nearby candelabra. I have no idea what I'm doing or where we're going, I just know I need to get him out of here.

"You're going to be quiet, or we'll *both* get into trouble. Do you understand?" He says nothing as his head bobs around. He may be too damaged. "I'm Amelvira, but you can call me Mel. My father is…" I pause, trying to rid him of the shackles on his wrist, rubbing them because I know how heavy they are. "He gets this way sometimes. Let's just say he won't remember you're here and his guards don't give a shit about Eva. They just like torturing you."

I don't know if what I'm saying is true. Over the years, I've seen them come down here, and with what I know of this place, I can safely assume they do my father's bidding in torturing whatever prisoners find themselves unlucky enough to be caged down here. I've overheard other guards saying Splint is known to leave people in them and Blaise has a fetish with setting fires no matter the object.

I help Silas from the chair, but he stumbles to his knees. He's heavy. He's lost most of the muscle in his body, but I'm so short that most of his upper body lies on top of my shoulders as I do my best to pick him up and keep him moving forward. "Do you know about karma? I have a strong feeling that Eva hasn't been returned because we have you here, but that doesn't mean I'm going to just let you go."

As I say the words, I hate them. They taste like bitter belladonna on my tongue, but I can't free him.

Never give anything without something in return.

It's so late that we pass no one up the stairs or down the halls. I toss him on Eva's bed and bring him a plate of food. He's already asleep, but I tell him anyway, "Food will be brought every morning. I'll release you once Eva's returned. Be grateful it's not the dungeon."

Father didn't remember Silas, but he did find me during one of his episodes the next day.

With Silas locked in Eva's room, there's no one to bring him food or release him. If he dies there… I can't think that way. I take a long pull of the dry rancid wine, long enough that my head feels like it's been replaced with stars in the night sky.

If I can survive another month of being forgotten, so can he.

Eva's home.

It's been two months since I released Silas, but Eva has finally been returned after a year of disappearance.

She showed up on our doorstep with stitches in her neck, her cheeks sunken in, her eyes bulging, and her skin inflamed, pink with irritation.

She's so small. Her arms look like sparring swords for children.

When I tried to hug her, she curled into herself and started weeping.

She won't look at me.

Her new guard, Maison, won't let anyone disturb her where she's held up in her room. So long as she has books, she's fine, but I still need to see her.

I wrote to Cain, as myself, but he refuses to come, claiming I'm lying just to get him home. I can't write as Eva, or that would prove him right even though he's wrong.

Maison is fine. I watch him and find that he picks out any apples that are on her plate before he brings it to her. He's also highly selective about what and who enters her room, meaning nothing he hasn't thoroughly combed through and no one.

Men are an absolute no. I started to like him when he turned away Mrs. Platewell for smelling too tarty. After another month of observing his patterns, I eventually understood what it took to break through his strong guard.

This morning, I put on a plain dress without any perfume and caked my face with makeup to look older than I am—*different*. When I approach him, he looks me over and smiles so wide his blue eyes twinkle.

"Come on, Maison," I trail my fingers up and down his arm.

He's so perfectly handsome, I'm surprised he's not a prince. He has a trusting look about him with an equally threatening form, which makes me more than grateful that Eva has him to protect her.

"What will it take for you to let me inside?"

Even his chuckle is charming.

"Look, Mel, you're a great observer. And because you saved Silas' life," he picks my hand up with his and kisses my knuckles, "I'll let you inside, but if she panics, you're out. Understood?"

I nod my head enthusiastically.

"Don't get any ideas about this, Princess. I'll be an engaged man soon."

I turn back on my heel and narrow my eyes. Guards don't marry. They're to give their lives to the throne. "What is her name?"

Oh, sweet Devine. I swear if he smiles at me like that again, I'm going to faint.

"Let's just say she's a quirky little do—"

"Maise!" Eva calls with a fear I've never heard her possess.

"Sorry, Princess, try again tomorrow?"

When he shuts the door, I head back to my room with a smile on my face. I may not have seen Eva, but I have someone else who is safe. He doesn't look at me with hunger in his eyes, and there's no way my father will send me to pull secrets from him when he's already under our roof.

Maison is safe.

It's been six months of getting to know Maison on my way to seeing Eva for a few minutes.

The day she's able to look at me again is the day Cain will tell me why he hates me. But I keep trying every day.

Maison's been encouraging her and helping me the best he can while teasing me over frivolous things like, "It's easier to run in pants," because I practically run toward him every day, and "Is the world different from down there?" because the top of my head literally comes to his chest.

The day I came strolling toward him in Cain's old leather riding pants and new heels, he looked at me, impressed. "That's one way to take a few comments from a nobody guard."

His smile was so sad that day. When I asked him what was wrong, he shook his head, took my palm, and placed a massive black ring in it. "It isn't worth anything, but it does open so you can keep something small in it."

"Why would you give this to me? Wait, is this——"

"It suits you better anyway. She's——" He shook his head, his blonde curls longer than when I first met him. "It's complicated."

With the heels, I didn't have to lift onto my toes to place a tender kiss on his cheek. "I'll never take it off."

Eventually, our conversations grew longer, and I told him everything. He had this aura about him that made me feel safe and seen. He was too good of a man to work for our family. When I told him about my marriage to Percival, and then the flirting my father forces me to do, he grew visibly angry. Something I missed about Cain—the care. He even hated hearing about people calling me devilish names.

The last thing he ever told me was, "You need to protect yourself, Princess. The world is a cruel place full of cunts, and you've already seen so much of it. Find the little things that bring you joy and own them. Never apologize for it. That's the only way to survive." His eyes lit up with an idea. "Has your sister ever wielded a weapon?"

"Eva? If books taught her anything, it's that princes do all the saving." He kissed my cheek and left.

That was the last time I saw him before he left me too.

Since then, Eva has started talking again and letting me into her room. Though it's still hard for her to look at me, I can see her trying. She's a ghost of her old self, but at least she's here. There aren't talks of books anymore, but daggers: the different sizes, handles, and blades.

A ball is too early for Eva. I knew it would be too early, but our father ordered us to come anyway, even though it's a false ball and we aren't supposed to.

Although they can't see the scar across her throat with the ruby choker she wears, they stare at her as if they can. That's not what they're looking at, though.

"Your sister is crazy," one of the princesses snickers in my direction. "Who is she talking to?"

Seeing my double in the corner, I rush toward her. "Sing." Her pretty face jumps to pure terror. "Forget it." I don't have time for someone to work through their own fear and dilemmas.

Clearing my throat, I take one of the young minstrel's hands and guide him to the dance floor. He holds more terror than Blair did, but he follows my lead anyway. "Name."

"Oliver."

"Sorry about this, Oliver." As we spin, I twist so fast, I hit three girls, and we all tumble to the ground. "Damn it, Oliver!" I shout. All eyes are on me, and I have to bite my smile seeing the snickering princess covered in cranberry juice.

It's Eva's silent laughter that makes my heart sing. Wiping myself down, I stand by her. "What do you say we make a little game of this mess?"

It's this moment that I understand what Maison was saying. Finding little joys in life is all I need. Making Eva smile and others angry is at the top of that list.

Seven Years Ago

Age Seventeen

My hands are ringing, my heart is pounding in my chest, and my stomach is in knots. It's been in knots for weeks, big, twisting knots that have me throwing up anything I eat or drink.

I know I'm pregnant. I don't know how to confirm it, but I know.

MALICIOUS INTENTIONS

Percival came to visit weeks ago. He was different—*angry*. When he took me over the dresser, it was like he was proving something, punishing me for something.

It was the best sex we've ever had, and by the end, he was still the soft, tender Percival he always is.

It's these moments I wish Cain didn't hate me, Maison hadn't disappeared, and Eva wasn't so solitary. Part of me is terrified, but this was always going to happen. We're married after all. We're supposed to bring heirs to this world.

Only, I don't want to share it—the baby, I mean. I'll share it with Percival, sure, but I don't want my father to get his hands on them. I want it all to myself. They won't be able to leave me because they'll be *mine*.

Since Cain ran off to the military and Eva is a recluse, I know Father will be proud. I'm waiting to tell him until my belly is fat. Until then, I'll pretend as if nothing is wrong. I'm just sick, is what I'll say. Mrs. Platewell's pork must have been rotten.

When I open my father's chambers, I sense something is amiss. Mrs. Platewell sees my entrance and takes it as her sign to leave. The slight shake in her head is all I need to know he's in an episode. She'll probably take him away tomorrow for a few months, so he doesn't hurt anyone.

When the door shuts, I jump. I didn't even notice the woman and man in the corner.

"You disappoint me, Rosebud. I thought…"

Fuck. Fuck. Fuck. Fuck. Fuck.

I turn to grab the door handle, but the cloaked woman steps in my way. "You thought I wouldn't find out about your affair. That you were pregnant with his child?!"

"No! Daddy, it's me, Amelvira!"

The glass he was holding shatters against the wall. Three steps pound toward me.

Smack!

Something wet covers my mouth and my vision blurs with my cries muffled until all I meet is a world of black.

My eyes are heavy. My mouth is dry. Pain sears down my middle as if I'm being cut in half.

"Take it all."

My eyes make out enough to know I'm in the dungeon. The cloaked woman is pretty from the side. Her brown hair and pointy nose make her look like a petite fairy.

"Just do it," she snaps. "King Aramos ordered it. He says he's had enough heirs."

Six Years Ago

Age Eighteen

My knee comes up hard between the man's legs. "Just because I touched your arm, doesn't mean I'll fuck you!"

Seducing people has become mundane, but this man really thought he could rip my dress from my body and hold me down to take what he wants because he told me he murdered his sister.

I run back to the ball, settle myself against the wall until my father comes into view, and motions me toward him. I follow him down another hall and into one of the rooms.

He looks irate, his cheeks are red, and his face is set in that stern way, but there isn't anything I've done that could warrant his anger, so it must be Eva or another deal gone bad.

When I enter the room, the door slams shut behind me. My arms are pulled back, and I'm thrown on the bed. Everything is so fast that I can't make sense of it until my hands are too tight above my head and my legs are pulled apart and secured in a way that won't let me close them. The cold, metal shackles dig into my skin.

My father's face comes inches from mine. I can smell the anger radiating from him. "You don't get to say no, Amelvira. You're my daughter. I gave you this body, you'll do what I say with it." He grips the neckline of my dress and rips until it's clean off. "You're going to lie here and let him finish."

I don't know why I need to. I got what he wanted; I got a secret. That's all my father ever wants. I've never had to go all the way with a man or woman because I get what I need before it comes to this.

"I know about the Trove."

"Fuck off, Mel. You don't know shit." Cain tosses his plate of eggs aside and leaves the table.

He thinks he's so sneaky, but I've gathered whispers from the men and women I've been with to connect a few pieces. I don't know much, but there are worried rumblings about certain people dying off in strange ways.

The Trove—that term has become like a myth. I don't know for sure that Cain is part of it, but it's something that would suit him.

And I want in.

Five Years Ago

Age Nineteen

Since Cain won't let me into the Trove, I've resorted to being useful in other ways, creating concoctions that have finally numbed me when I need it. *Serenade snuff*, I call it. I've made pixie powder that makes others hyper and a dream draught to put someone to sleep.

Eva won't let me help her though.

Last week, she ran into the woods and nearly killed herself. She swears she keeps seeing a white-faced man she's begun calling the *Phantom*, but every time she tries to show him to me, there's no one there.

Father has doctors and has even consulted a witch, but they all say she's hearing voices and seeing things that aren't there.

My heart shattered overhearing that. If she's like Father, I fear she'll never get the happy ending she's dreamed of, or worse, she'll hurt someone.

Two Years Ago

Age Twenty-two

MALICIOUS INTENTIONS

Following Cain is easy.

He's so cocky, he thinks he's untouchable, but I'm determined to find out why he came back and why he's decided to reclaim his role as heir. He's made it his life's mission to make Father red in the face every chance he gets, claiming he'll never wed or have children.

Then, this morning, he met with Father for less than five minutes before leaving abruptly. I overheard him announce that he'll marry, and to ensure the false prince's ball is a masquerade set a year from now.

My gut instinct told me to follow him, and here I am, scoping out a sizable manor set deep in the woods.

Either way, I'll be taking him off guard, so I start toward the door with only a sliver of hope that he won't slam it in my face.

"Cain's wicked sister is quite resourceful," a deep, grumbly voice calls behind me. The man I see leaning against a tree is huge with black ink and brutal scars that cover most of his body. There's a white bandage wrapped around his middle, and I can see he's working to stand up right.

I plant my palm on my hip with my chin high. "Name."

A subtle smirk lifts up one side of his face, a dimple forming with it. "You can call me Duke." He nods behind me. "And that's Dove."

The moment I turn around, the old woman's mouth parts, a frown etching deep into her withered skin. Her eyes, though... They're so young for someone so old.

"What's your problem?"

"Your eyes." She shakes her head as if ridding the image from her mind.

"A bad omen." I roll mine. "I've heard it all. What is it you prefer? Satan's Spawn? Wicked Witch? Mistress of all evil?"

"Distraction," Duke says, rounding to Dove's side. "Your reputation is notable. We could use someone as skilled at creating diversions as you."

He heads into the house and motions for me to follow. My stomach jumps as high as I feel. That was easy.

Dove grabs my arm before I can make it across the threshold. "Your reputation *is* known. Don't think you can fuck your way into this group."

I yank my arm from her hold. "If you want me to stay away from him, just say so. All you've done is make me want to bend over a table and let him have his way with me."

I give her a wink and head inside.

She's just become my newest challenge. I won't fuck Duke, but I'll get Dove to like me one day.

One Year Ago

Twenty-three

I'm an adult, yet here I am, dancing in red, hot shoes with my sister because my brother wed a harlot. The same harlot my father ordered me to bed. I didn't know it was Audrey, *the* Audrey my brother lost long ago.

"You won't follow his footsteps," my father barks.

It's cruel that I'm already married and have to be taught this lesson, but I'd have thrown them on and danced with Eva even if he didn't order me to.

Whatever distraction the Trove needs tomorrow is going to be difficult, but I never fail at what they ask for. A disastrous speech so they can sneak into a castle, seduce a guard, release horses, and pretend to break my ankle. It's been fun, but they still won't give me a mask or trust me with any of their real identities, except Cain obviously.

"Stop," my father orders. Eva and I fall to our knees and toss the shoes in the corner with heavy breaths.

"You'll both be attending Princess Aspen's ball next week." He looks at Eva as if they share a secret I don't know about before turning to me. "Then it's the Deimos Kingdom. Your doubles are to wed soon."

Relief spreads through every inch of me.

It's finally over.

ACKNOWLEDGMENTS

First, I cannot believe we have a third book in the Cruel Kingdoms series. This entire novella series snowballed into what it is today because of everyone who laid their eyes on the early drafts of Sinister Desire and provided all of their feedback. If someone hadn't said they wanted Cain's POV, there would have been no Trove, Duke, and possibly the rest of the series as it's unfolded thus far.

So, the biggest acknowledgement of all will forever be my alpha and beta readers! Those who help us indie authors by reading our early drafts and give us their honest feedback and thoughts should never go unrecognized. Every positive and "negative" opinion helps tremendously, and I couldn't be more grateful to have met each and every one of you:

AJ Bryce, Valeria Jiun, Kim Bobbitt, Riley Carlson, Stacey Biller, Brittney Rivera, Jackie Marie, Beth B., Bristin, Tequilla, Fiona, and Sky (hazybee_reads).

I also can't forget Na'ysha! Your artwork is incredible, and I couldn't be more thankful for all the work you do bringing these characters to life!

Shout out to all the ARC readers who signed up, not just for Malicious Intensions, but Sinister Desire and Fateful Chance as well. It's because of you all that we're able to get our stories further into the world!

Special thanks to Bristin! I've said it before and I will absolutely be singing this to the world; you are such an incredible person. Your chaos and positivity go hand and hand and are truly admirable.

Shayla! You absolutely got bombarded with this book as I started to gather all my thoughts and outlines, so huge thank you for being on the receiving end of that and for being such a huge support.

Geena, you beautiful soul, I will love and adore you forever! There's only one other person who could handle my hyper focused ramblings...

Nadia, your patience needs to be studied. Your genuine interest in my jumbled thoughts fills my heart.

Nick! Thanks for giving me your last name. It looks so good on these books.